Spring Break

She knelt and placed her hand on the red-brown fur that had gotten Brandy his name. The body was cold. At first there didn't seem to be a mark on the dog until Angie reached out and lifted his head. A thin line of dark, clotted blood made a necklace across Brandy's throat.

Ghosts don't slit dog's throats.

The thought came uninvited. Was there a connection to the crying in the attic and Brandy's death? Were they going to find the others killed in a similar manner?

Also by Barbara Steiner

The Mummy
The Phantom

Point Horror

SPRING BREAK

Barbara Steiner

■SCHOLASTIC

Scholastic Children's Books,
Commonwealth House, 1-19 New Oxford Street,
London, WC1A 1NU, UK
a division of Scholastic Publications Ltd
London ~ New York ~ Toronto ~ Sydney ~ Auckland

First published in the US by Scholastic Inc., 1996
First published in the UK by Scholastic Ltd, 1997

Copyright © Barbara Steiner, 1996

ISBN: 0 590 19034 2

All rights reserved

Printed by Cox & Wyman, Reading, Berks

10 9 8 7 6

Chapter 1

"We've escaped!" Angie Hendrix jumped into the backseat of her best friend Kerry Cole's old Jeep and sighed deeply. "I can't believe it."

"No more teachers, no more books." Paula Lantz sang the popular jingle as they headed south out of some unreal Saturday morning Houston traffic. She leaned her head of mahogany-red curls into Angie's shoulder and whispered, "Change seats with me at the next light."

Angie looked at Paula, shrugged, and announced, "Change seats with me, Paula. I want the best view. I want to be sure that we're really getting out of the city for a week."

At the next stoplight, both girls snapped off their seat belts and made a quick exchange of seating.

Paula squeezed Angie's arm and sang again. "In the meantime, in between time . . . That's what we're in. In between time. I don't want to hear one word this week about s-c-h-o-o-l."

"Don't you even want to talk about what we'll do this summer?" Kerry looked at Paula and Angie in the rearview mirror. "Let's get jobs in Estes Park. Colorado in the summer is heaven on earth."

"You can't do that, Kerry." Kerry's boyfriend spoke for the first time. Chad Grindle wasn't exactly a morning person. He wasn't even an afternoon person. He came alive for evening football games and after-school basketball practice. Angie had never known a guy with so much athletic ability.

He certainly was the opposite of Angie's brother, Justin. Justin sat on the other side of Paula with his nose in a book about identifying birds on the coast of Texas.

Chad continued to stare at Kerry and protest. "I already have a job in Houston. You can't go off someplace for the summer."

"You could get a job in Colorado, too." Kerry tapped her fingers as they waited for yet another red light.

"I couldn't get a vet job. You know I have

to work at the veterinary clinic for a couple of summers in order to get into vet school. They want you to know what being a vet is really like. They want to know you're serious."

At the sound of Chad's voice, Brandy, his chocolate Labrador retriever, jumped up from where he was tucked into the front-seat floor and barked.

Angie glanced at Justin. How could he read with all this commotion and excitement about going to the beach for spring break? He was totally inhuman.

"Watch it, Paula. The real reason I wanted to change places is that Justin gets carsick when he tries to read and ride in the backseat."

"You're kidding." Paula made a funny face and leaned away from Justin. "I thought only little kids did that."

"Justin is your problem, Angie. You're the one who had to have a chaperon in order to go with us. You'll have to clean up the mess." Kerry laughed and peeled onto Highway 45 leading to Galveston.

Angie grinned and kept her mouth shut. Kerry was right. She'd had a devil of a time talking her parents into letting her take this trip.

Going to the beach for spring break was

Kerry's idea. She could talk her parents into anything. Both her mother and dad thought Kerry Cole could do no wrong, but secretly, Angie thought they both were afraid of Kerry. Well, maybe not afraid, but in awe of her.

Who wouldn't be? Angie stared at the back of Kerry's perfect long, thick blonde hair that curled just the right amount. She was in awe of Kerry, too. Even though they had been best friends forever, Angie never got over looking at Kerry and thinking how beautiful she was. How smart. How perfect. And to top it off, how mechanical.

Kerry, herself — well, maybe her father had helped her a little — had worked on the engine of the Jeep. She and her dad had cleaned up and painted the body until it looked brand-new. They'd hired someone to have the interior restored, but Kerry had earned the money to pay for it working in her dad's body shop.

Angie sighed audibly. Some people have multiple talents and gifts. Angie had Justin.

"Does your brother do anything *but* read?" Paula asked, interrupting Angie's thinking.

"Why don't you ask me?" Justin said, still looking at his book. "I'm within hearing distance of you."

"Oh, he talks, he walks, he — "

Angie interrupted Paula. "He writes in his journal. And in those notebooks. He has about a million notebooks by now. He plans to write the great American novel."

Everyone continued to joke and talk. The more they laughed, the more Brandy barked. Chad placed his hand on the lab's head to quiet him.

"Can I change my mind, guys?" Justin said. "If it's going to be this noisy all week, I'll lose it."

"Poor baby." Angie stopped laughing. She had argued and argued, but her mother said no way was she going out of town for a week with three high school kids. Did dear old Mom think Justin was an adult because he was eighteen and graduating in May? Technically, he was still a "high school kid." Little did her mom know that once they got to the island, Justin would have his nose in a book all the time. He'd no more watch after Angie than Brandy would.

She griped and complained to Kerry and Paula, but they didn't care if Justin went. In fact, for some odd reason, Paula was happy Justin was going.

The highway grew more and more congested. As they crossed the bay to the island, the bridge turned into a parking lot. It took nearly an hour to get over to the island resort.

"Think we'll find a place to stay?" Chad asked, voicing the concern all of them felt as they sat and watched gulls soar and dive for scraps of bread people tossed them from the cars.

"Sure. We'll find *something*," Angie said.

She didn't care where they stayed, as long as they were away from school and on the beach.

"I love you, Kerry," Angie announced when the car finally started to move after one long gridlock. "This is the best idea you *ever* had, and you've had some beauts."

"Ditto," Paula said. "Did you hear about the blondes on spring break who saw a sign saying 'Disney World, left.' They were disappointed but turned around and went back home."

Kerry, used to Paula's "dumb blonde" jokes, swung the loaded car to the right and headed out Road 3005.

Justin groaned. "I'm not going to be able to handle this, Angie. Are all your friends this intelligent?"

Their laughing and joking lasted only a short time longer. Then reality set in. By late afternoon, they had passed Jamaica Beach, stopping at every place they could find that looked as if it might have rooms for rent, but there were no vacancies. They stopped at three real estate offices, asking about houses for the week, cabins, shacks, closets. No luck. Every teen in Texas must already be in Galveston. Colleges were having spring break, too.

"Why didn't anyone make a reservation?" Chad asked. "We've known we were coming for two weeks."

"I didn't think it would be this crowded." Kerry leaned on the Jeep's fender and twisted a curl around her finger. They were now at the end of the island.

"Okay, people, shape up." Justin took charge. "Let's go in that little store across the street and get some supplies. We did bring camping gear." He started in the direction of a small general store, probably the last place to stock up before they reached the more isolated beaches.

"I hate camping!" Kerry stood up straight and put her hands on her hips.

"Me, too." Paula started after Justin. "But it looks as if we have no choice."

Chad whistled for Brandy, who'd been so glad to get out of the car that he'd run away up the block, sniffing every bush.

The woman in the store was shaking her head as Angie and Paula stepped inside. "People are probably getting good money for closets and garages by now," she said in answer to Justin's query about housing.

"You can't think of anything?" Angie begged.

"Well, I do know of one place." She rubbed her chin as if it helped her think. "Eldon Minor has been working on the old Jamison place for almost a year now. It might be in good enough shape to live in. If you aren't particular."

"We're not choosy at all," Paula said.

"I'll call him for you. He lives right down the road, when he's home." The pleasant-faced woman picked up a phone and dialed. She waited for it to ring. "There is one problem with the house."

"That figures." Angie felt her hopes slide. "There would be a catch. What is it?"

"Some people around here say the place is haunted."

The five friends looked at each other, and for once, no one could think of anything to say.

Chapter 2

Angie finally broke the silence. "Haunted? You have to be kidding."

"There're no such things as ghosts — are there?" Kerry tried to laugh, but she moved closer to Chad.

"Oooohhhhh." Chad raised his arms in a menacing motion toward Kerry. Then he grabbed and hugged her. "If there are, I'll protect you."

"Hey, guys, renting the house might be fun." Justin grinned. "I can write some ghost stories when I get home."

"You do that, Edgar Allan." Paula shook her head. "Maybe we can find you some ravens out there while we're at it."

"There is a bird sanctuary near the old house," the woman behind the counter said, ignoring Paula's reference to Poe's famous poem. "The place is fairly isolated — for beach property. Never saw so much development as we've had in the last few years. Despite the hurricanes, people seem to want to live out here."

"You aren't expecting a hurricane this week, are you?" Paula was through being funny for a few minutes.

"Oh, no, too early in the season. But I think rain is predicted by the end of the week." She started bagging their purchases.

"Then we'd better not worry about ghosts," Chad decided. "A roof over our heads is our number-one priority."

"Where did you say we can we find this Mr. Minor?" Kerry asked.

"Let me call him back. The line was busy, so he's there. . . . Eldon? Myra Adams here. Some young people want to rent the old Jamison place. You made much progress at getting it livable?" She listened and nodded.

"She looks positive," Angie whispered to Kerry. "Let's go talk him into renting. Surely he'd like the money if he's fixing it up."

Mrs. Adams smiled and nodded. "He said yes if you aren't too particular. I told him you weren't. I didn't say desperate. The old fool will try for more money."

"Is the electricity on?" Kerry asked.

"Sure. Everything works out there, but if I were you, I'd take some drinking water with you. Pipes are probably old and haven't been used much."

Justin lifted four gallons of spring water onto the counter and paid for it. Chad and Paula gathered their groceries, while Kerry got directions to Eldon Minor's house.

"Think we're doing the right thing?" Kerry asked Angie.

"Of course. And besides, what choice have we got? We're lucky to find anything." Angie slid into the car, hoping for the best.

She wasn't quite so sure when she met Eldon Minor. He was a creepy little old man, all hunched over, with a permanent crick in his neck. He had only a fringe of hair left around his neck and ears. His face was long and thin, and his ears must have belonged to someone else at one time. They were much too big for his own face. His eyes were a faded blue, but they had a little sparkle left. He smiled a crooked smile at them.

"Sure you want to stay out there?" he asked again. "Pretty far from town, and no near neighbors."

"Then no one will complain if we play loud

music or stay up late partying, will they?" Chad laughed.

"I may be out there working a lot if the weather holds," Eldon warned. "I don't mind a little noise, though. Just so you don't disturb my birds."

"Your birds?" Paula raised her eyebrows and looked at Angie.

"Well, they ain't mine, but I like 'em to feel comfortable living in that marsh behind my property. Might be some migrants from Mexico this time of year, too. You like birds?"

The five looked at each other. Did they have to answer that they liked birds to get the rental? "I do," Justin answered for them. "Are there a lot of varieties?"

"You'll be surprised." Eldon gathered some tools and prepared to leave.

"Any ravens?" Paula asked, avoiding Justin's eyes.

"Well, might be, but more likely waders." He headed for his truck, motioning for them to follow, but then stopped and stared at the Jeep. "Nice car."

"Thanks." Kerry shrugged and hopped into the driver's seat. She put the Jeep into gear and crept along behind Eldon Minor.

"Waders?" Angie asked, picturing birds with

rubber boots on, carefully stepping into the surf.

"He's the birdman of Galveston," Paula quipped. "Do we like birds? I'm sure."

"I have nothing against birds," Kerry said with a grin.

Kerry had no trouble following all the bends and turns of the beach road, since Eldon drove about twenty miles per hour.

"Jeez, look at that," Angie said, hanging out the side window.

The first view of the old Jamison house in the fading light made her think it deserved a ghost. Why had someone built such a huge mansion this far out of town and so near the ocean?

"I'd be disappointed if it *wasn't* haunted." Justin stood up for a better look.

"You're good with words, Justin," Paula said. "Describe this place."

"Well, it's three-story, kind of square, except for the trimmed-off corners on either side of the roof. I'll bet there's a big room behind that dormer in front with the rounded window and the deck."

"That's not a deck, it's a balcony. There are balconies all across the front of each story," Angie added, not able to keep her mouth shut.

"What fun to sit out there and look at the ocean."

"Maybe it was once a small hotel," Chad said.

"Or a sanatorium." Kerry pulled in beside Eldon Minor's truck at the front of the house.

"Oh, not a hospital, please," Paula said. "Not with all that — that fancy trim."

Any paint left on the house was peeling badly, leaving a silvery sheen where winds off the ocean had weathered the wood.

"The house is lonely," Angie said, without meaning to.

"Houses don't have feelings, Angie." Justin stepped out of the car behind her. "That's your imagination."

"Did I imagine that a curtain moved just now — on the second floor, to the left?" Kerry clutched Chad's arm.

"Surely you did. No one is supposed to be out here." Chad called to Eldon Minor, who had finally gotten out of his truck, "Anyone living here now, Mr. Minor?"

"Nope. Not for years. That's why I bought it cheap. All the furnishings came with it, too, but they're old and not very fancy.

"Do you think the house is haunted?" Paula asked.

"He-he-he." The man's laugh turned into a wheeze, then a coughing fit. "That what Myra told you?" he said finally.

"You don't charge extra for ghosts, do you?" Paula said, heading for the trunk to get her suitcase.

They struck a deal with Eldon Minor, a lot less money than they'd thought they'd have to pay for a place to sleep, which pleased them. He took them inside and showed them the fuse box, the switch to the water pump, everything he thought they'd need to know in an emergency.

Angie let the guys and Kerry take the technical tour. She hung back and started upstairs. She looked at the central staircase that split on the first landing, sending a separate set of steps to the right and left. The stairs were covered with old carpet, richly patterned in purple and blue, now faded in the center to lavender and heather. Turkish or Persian, surely expensive. Who would haunt a house so richly elegant at one time? And why was the house abandoned? Who left so abruptly, leaving all their furniture, even photographs and paintings, behind?

The biggest question, though, was, did she

really want to go up to the second floor by herself?

When Angie reached the first landing, a rush of shivers slid up and down her body and her legs froze in place. She clutched the railing and waited for the chill to go away.

Slowly she was able to back down, never taking her eyes off the closed doors to the rooms she could see. Had there been someone — or *something* — in one of the front rooms watching them arrive? Was it still there?

Angie was sure she was just being silly, but she'd wait until they all went up together to explore. That was for sure. Shaking off the spell she was under, she turned and flew back to the sound of voices in the kitchen wing of the house.

She took Paula's arm. "Let's all sleep in one room — the girls, I mean."

"Suits me." Paula looked at Angie. "You look as if you've already seen the ghost. Did you go upstairs by yourself?"

"No, I couldn't. I went part way and backed out. The place is just so big. I mean, we could have brought half the junior class with us."

"Go get your suitcase, and then we'll go up and pick a room." Paula had brought her suitcase in already. But she waited to go upstairs until Angie had come back.

"See, you didn't go up there by yourself, either. Come on." Angie practically ran up the staircase now that she wasn't alone.

The first bedroom that faced the ocean was huge, plenty big enough for three people. "Look, there are still beds here. Wouldn't you think whoever moved out would have taken their furniture?" Angie sat on one bed, testing the mattress. The covers sent up a musty smell and felt slightly damp, as if morning fog had come inside and never left.

"I think this was some sort of rooming house," Paula said. "I'm going to put my sleeping bag on the mattress. No telling who slept here last."

"It's so damp in here." Angie pulled her shoulders up to her ears and hugged herself. Then she jumped up and ran to check the view.

Angie pushed open the double doors with full-length glass panes that led to a small balcony.

"Paula, come out here. Oh, look."

There was enough light left to see navy-blue swells starting way out, turn green closer to shore, and then become foamy white surf as water slid onto the beach. Angie would have thought she was in paradise if Eldon Minor hadn't chosen that time to come out the front door. He stood looking up at her and grinning. Leering was more like it.

Angie didn't know Paula had come out onto the balcony until she spoke quietly. "He gives me the creeps," Paula said. "I hope he won't hang around all week."

"Let's wave to remind him he was leaving." Angie stretched her mouth into as big a smile as possible and waved her hand back and forth. "Bye. Thanks. And don't worry about us. We'll be fine out here."

He took the hint and crawled into his truck cab. Angie and Paula watched until his taillights disappeared.

"Thank goodness he's gone," Kerry said, coming in with her own bag. "This is great." She plunked down her suitcase and set her portable CD-tape-radio player on the old maple dresser against the wall opposite her bed. She unzipped her smaller bag and tugged her swimsuit from the top layer. "Let's go swimming before it's pitch dark."

"Chad and Brandy are already in the water." Angie pulled Kerry out to see the view off the balcony.

The three girls watched Chad throw a Frisbee up the beach for Brandy. The dog often caught it before it hit the ground.

"Last one in's a — " Angie stopped her dare in mid-sentence. "Listen . . ."

Paula grabbed Angie's arm on one side, Kerry's on the other. The three stood in the doorway of the bedroom, listening.

Then the music started. Not a proper, eerie tune, suitable for a haunted house. But dance music, party music. And faintly, behind and between the notes, came the sound of someone laughing.

Chapter 3

"Do ghosts laugh?" Paula asked in a whisper.

"I — I think ghosts can do anything they want to do." Angie knew very little about ghosts, and that was fine with her.

"What should we do?" Kerry was about to squeeze Angie's arm off. Her face was pale, and she was shaking.

"All we can do is leave," Angie decided. "Do we want to turn around and go back to town, or go find a place to camp?"

"I don't." Paula stood on her bed, listening, since the sounds in the attic had stopped. "We'll stick really close together and see if it happens again."

"We'll stay outside as much as possible." Kerry took a deep breath and agreed. "We were going to do that anyway."

"Okay, let's get out of here now and tell the

guys what we heard." Angie opened her bag and pulled out her swimsuit. "I hope they won't laugh at us."

Angie, Paula, and Kerry changed into swimsuits and were on the beach in nothing flat. By the time they got there, they felt foolish and agreed not to mention what they'd heard — or thought they'd heard — in the old house.

The stretch of sand that ran parallel to the Jamison mansion was a vacationer's dream. Deserted for as far as they could see, the sand was clean as was the water. Not far back from the beach ran an area with dunes and thick saltwater grasses.

The marsh that Eldon Minor said was a bird sanctuary must have been farther north. Occasionally a long-legged bird lifted off and drifted toward the ocean. The air was still, the dusk incredibly quiet. They heard a few bird sounds, just the hiss and splash of the surf in its rhythm of up and back, up and back.

Angie, Kerry, and Paula needed noise. They giggled and shouted and screamed, running and splashing and swimming in the vanishing light. Angie squealed and laughed, getting rid of any leftover fear from being in the house and hearing the unexpected music.

Two seagulls hovered overhead, squawking, adding to the human chaos. Angie stopped once, watching Paula and Kerry, wondering if they, too, were squealing and screaming a little extra to get rid of the fear that had washed over all of them earlier? She glanced at the house. It seemed to be watching them.

"Quoth the seagull, nevermore. Right, Justin?" Paula chased after him, pushing him down into the surf.

Angie was both surprised and pleased to see her ultraserious brother laugh, act silly, and relax for a change.

."You don't believe in ghosts, do you, Justin? Seriously?" Angie asked her brother as they walked slowly back to the house to start dinner.

Justin grinned at Angie. "As a matter of fact, I do. I've done a lot of reading on the subject."

Paula looked at Angie and made a face. "Spirits hanging around because they're unhappy, that stuff?"

"Yes, but I read about a woman who knew her son was visiting when she smelled roses. He always gave her roses for Mother's Day and Valentine's."

"So there can be nice ghosts?" Kerry joined in the conversation. "Ghosts that laugh?" She was wrapped in a huge orange and red striped beach towel as if she were cold, and Chad had his arm around her.

"Ghosts aren't always menacing." Justin smiled at Paula, making Angie realize that her brother was actually flirting with her friend. This was interesting — but strange. She'd always ignored Justin or thought of him as a super dweeb.

"We heard something." Angie decided to tell the guys about their experience. "From upstairs, where you said there was a room behind the dormer windows."

Chad laughed. "What did you hear? Moaning and groaning?"

"No." Kerry frowned at him. "We heard music, all three of us, so we know we weren't making it up."

"What kind of music?" Justin stared at Paula.

"I think it was the Doobie Brothers." She grinned and looked away.

"The Doobie Brothers?" Chad laughed and pushed Kerry. Then he whipped off his towel and popped her with it. "These *women* are trying to scare us, Justin. Are we going to allow that?"

"I don't know who was playing. Just some obscure rock band," Paula said. "I didn't recognize the song, and we didn't stay around long after we heard it, but we really did hear music. And laughter. We're not making this up."

"We're not kidding," Angie added, afraid the guys didn't believe them. If she had been the only one, she could have thought she was nuts. But three people don't imagine something at the same time.

"Okay, I'll believe you," Justin conceded. "But next time you hear it, come get me. This is fascinating."

"Sure it is. So is serial murder and vampires and — "

"Dinner." Chad cut Paula off. "I'm starving. Did we have lunch?"

"I think you only had two Big Macs and a double order of fries." Kerry punched him. "You must be fading away by now."

Angie started to run. "Last one in the kitchen has to do dishes." Getting dressed, fixing dinner, normal things — these were easier to think about than ghost bands. She needed to move and keep busy.

They used the pots and pans they'd brought for camping, banging them around, making a lot of noise. They were pleased that the old gas stove worked. In no time they heated water for spaghetti and poured sauce from a jar for the topping. Kerry chopped veggies for a salad. Angie buttered the big loaf of French bread they'd bought at Myra's store.

The kitchen was cozy, and they were stuffed and mellow when they heard the music again.

"There! Hear it?" Angie froze over the sink where she was scrubbing the spaghetti pot. Her hand squeezed into the S.O.S pad until it scratched her fingers. She had to consciously let go of it and shake her hand.

The sound was faint, but everyone heard it this time.

"I think it's coming from upstairs someplace," Justin said. "Let's check it out."

"Check it out?" Angie wasn't sure that was first on her agenda. "Maybe — maybe — "

"You want to hide someplace until it goes away, wimp?" Justin said just the right thing to make Angie feel foolish if she said no. He was good at that.

Actually, Angie had a reputation for being the daring one in her crowd. She was first off the diving board, first off the ski lift when they took vacations in Colorado, first on the big, advanced hills. In a day or two, she'd be the one to say, let's see how far out we can swim without stopping.

But first in line for a ghost hunt? That was different.

"Okay, let me get my flashlight," she conceded.

She led the way upstairs, taking them two at a time.

"The sound *is* on the third floor," Angie said, now willing to be the leader, since she had company. "There must be a staircase someplace."

For a time they were stumped. No door along the hall of the second floor opened onto stairs leading upward. "In this big a place, they must have had servants," Justin finally said. "Let's go back to the kitchen."

"Of course. A back stairway to the servants' quarters." Angie found the door in the walk-in pantry. She was a fan of English mysteries and gothic romances. There was always a back staircase.

The passageway was narrow, steep, and twisting, just like in the movies. The five huddled together on the landing.

"This must be the second floor," Angie whispered. "I can't believe there's no door."

"Privacy. Maids used the main staircase during the day to clean." Kerry grabbed and squeezed Angie's hand. "Are we crazy going up here or what?"

"I'll protect you." They heard the sound of toenails on the steps behind them. Chad laughed. "So will Brandy. Good boy. Come on, sniff out the bad guys."

Angie felt claustrophobic and started up again, letting each step feel solid under her foot before she put her weight down. The stairs opened onto a hall that led to several small rooms on the west wing of the third floor. Without the big windows and doors of the main rooms, the area smelled musty and unused.

Dust filled Angie's nostrils and she stifled a sneeze. Somehow it seemed important to stay quiet.

And it was quiet now, deathly quiet. Occasionally a board one of them stepped on would creak, but no music surrounded them. Not one note.

They didn't find a light in the hall, and the darkness was as black as inside a cave deep in the ground. Angie spotted Justin running his hands along the wall at the top of the stairs. "I wonder if this was sealed off at some time," he whispered.

"Why would anyone do that?" Paula helped

him search for bumps or a crack, but they found nothing.

"There must be another way in if there's a room behind this wall." Angie let her light play along the top of the wall and the ceiling.

Chad's stomach growled and they would have laughed, would have abandoned their search of the third floor, if Brandy hadn't crouched in front of the wall whining. If the music hadn't started up again.

This time, soft music, dreamy music.

And voices.

First a female voice, softly arguing.

Then a child's voice, insistent, begging.

Then soft weeping, crying that gradually turned to sobbing, tragic, heartbroken sobs.

Chapter 4

"Who is it?" Kerry whispered. "That's not a ghost. That's someone real."

Chad knocked on the wall. "Anyone there?" he shouted. "Can we help you?"

Brandy jumped up, putting his feet on the wall, and barked his own question, catching the mood of them all — half excitement, half fear.

All noises stopped abruptly. The five huddled together, listening. They heard nothing else.

"Maybe there's another way into the room," Angie said softly. "Let's go find it."

"Let's *not*." Paula had heard enough. Lightly running, she started downstairs and everyone followed, not wanting to be left alone in the dark at the top of the stairs.

In the kitchen, Angie spoke. "But if someone needs help — "

Paula interrupted her. "If someone needed help, he or she would have said so when Chad knocked on the wall. Ghosts don't need help."

"You really think it's a ghost, don't you?" Angie tried to decide what she believed.

"I don't know what to think. I think a cup of cocoa would taste great." Paula headed for the stove. She poured water from one of their bottles into a saucepan and put it on to heat.

Angie got out their cups and put a couple of heaping spoonfuls of instant cocoa into each cup. No one spoke.

"Okay." Kerry broke the silence. "Do you think we should pack up and leave?"

Chad spoke first. "Why should we do that? No one is bothering us. I'd say we might be bothering them, maybe by just being here."

"I don't know about you guys, but hearing something I don't understand bothers me," Paula said. "Especially hearing someone crying."

"But you didn't want to do anything about it. You didn't want to see if we could find the room and get inside." Chad took his cocoa, holding his hands over the steaming liquid as if he were cold.

Justin shrugged. "Where's your sense of humor, Paula? We found the only place left in Galveston to rent, and now we find out why it was cheap and still available. It really is haunted. Isn't that funny?"

A tiny smile crept over Paula's face. "Okay, okay, this *is* funny. This is a really hilarious situation we find ourselves in."

Chad picked up his cup with one hand and pulled Kerry to her feet with the other. "Let's go sit on the beach and watch the stars, Ker. These people have forgotten why we left town for spring break."

Angie watched Chad put his arm around Kerry and Kerry snuggle into his shoulder. She felt a twinge of — of — well, jealousy. She was used to Chad being around, Chad's arm around Kerry. Maybe what she felt was loneliness.

Then Justin made her feel worse. He pulled Paula into the chair at the table beside him. "You don't think all the world is funny, do you, Paula? What are you hiding from?"

"What do you mean, Justin?" Paula said defensively.

"I've known people like you before. They joke all the time to cover up a lot of real feelings."

To Angie's surprise, and, she was sure, to Paula's dismay, Paula burst into tears. That gave Justin reason to pull her even closer for a long hug.

What was happening? Just because they'd heard some unexplainable sounds, Chad and Kerry were escaping and her brother was acting like a human being, actually being an understanding person — and possibly falling for Paula. And Angie was feeling sorry for herself.

She had imagined their sitting around a fireplace every night playing the games they'd brought. Going for late-night swims, or playing on the beach.

It never once occurred to her that Justin and Paula would pair off, leaving her odd man out, the third wheel on a mountain bike. Gloom settled deeper as the similes kept coming. Three peas in a pod. Tea for three. Three's a crowd. . . .

She grabbed her cocoa and hurried upstairs before anyone could see the tears spilling down her cheeks. Good grief.

She pulled on her old flannel nightgown and crawled into bed, propping herself up with two pillows. Sipping the sweet chocolate liquid, she tried to read. It was so quiet here, too quiet.

She opened the double doors onto the balcony so she could hear the rhythm of the tide, which should have relaxed her. It didn't. The *whoosh* and *shush* sounded like whispering, like the ocean calling to her. "Angie!" She scolded her wild imagination.

She turned out the light and stepped out onto the balcony, determined to enjoy the sound of water in her front yard. She refused to wonder, or imagine, what her friends were doing. The images came anyway.

Kerry and Chad were snuggled together on the beach, sipping their hot chocolate and exchanging kisses.

Justin was listening to Paula pour out the sad circumstances of her home life. Angie knew how Paula's father ruled with an iron hand, how Paula and her mother were both afraid of him. Her mother was unhappy but afraid to leave, since someone had always taken care of her. Paula counted the days until she could escape. Her jokes were all cover for real feelings. Justin read through her funnygirl act sooner than most people did. Angie realized she didn't know her brother as well as she'd thought.

"Psssst. Psssst."

It took Angie a few seconds to realize that she heard a sound other than the ocean's whisper.

She gripped the balcony rail, making her hands into claws around the peeling wood. "What?"

"Pssst. Pssst. Who are you? Welcome."

She whirled around, looked both ways. Why had she turned off her bedside lamp before she stepped onto the balcony? The whisper came from inside the house, but the bedroom was a black hole. She couldn't even see the doorway — until slowly, slowly the French door swung shut and clicked.

"Hey!" Angie ran to the door. She twisted the knob. The door was locked.

Chapter 5

She ran down the balcony to the next bed-room; she was just barely able to make out the door in the darkness, using her hands to search. She twisted that knob. Locked.

Shivering by now, chilled by both the night air and the whispers, Angie dashed back to the rail in front of her bedroom.

"Chad! Kerry!" She yelled as loud as she could. Would they hear her voice over the sound of the waves? She wasn't even sure they were on the beach in front of the house. They might have walked along the shore. "Help!"

She glanced behind her. Who had whispered to her? Was he — she — still there? *Someone* had moved inside to lock the door. She turned to face the ocean again.

Paula and Justin would never hear her. And she couldn't get to the balcony on the other side of the second floor. A bulge and a window where the stairway ran separated the two second-floor balconies.

"Chad! Kerry!" She yelled again. "Help! Please, help!"

"Angie?" Kerry's voice was soft below her, on the lawn. "Angie, what's wrong?"

"I'm locked out of the bedroom. Oh, Kerry, please come upstairs and let me in." Angie collapsed in tears. Maybe it was realizing that someone had finally heard her.

She sat and waited, huddled in a ball, her back to the rail, her knees drawn up to her chin. She pulled her flannel gown tight to her legs and tucked it under her bare feet.

Lights came on inside. The door popped open. Kerry ran out, laughing. "Angie, why did you think you were locked out on the balcony? This door opened easily. You must be freezing." Kerry helped Angie to her feet and led her back into the freezing bedroom. She pushed Angie into her sleeping bag and pulled the blankets from the bed around her.

Angie savored the covers, not caring if the wool smelled musty and damp. She put her head down on her knees, pushing her fingers against her temples, trying to gain her composure.

Angie finally spoke. "Someone shut me outside there. A voice whispered, and then I thought they locked the balcony door."

"What voice?" Paula and Justin had followed Chad and Kerry upstairs.

"I don't know *what* voice." Angie's hands on the rough wool made fists. She took a deep breath before she spoke again. Don't bite the hand that rescues you. "It was a real person. I know that."

"I think you're tired, baby sister." Justin grinned and pulled Paula out the door into the hall. Angie heard Paula giggle, and then heard them run back downstairs.

"I know you didn't make this up," Kerry said after Chad had left.

"At least someone believes me," Angie said. "I'm sorry to mess up your evening."

"Don't worry, Angie. I'm really tired, I hardly slept last night from packing and then excitement. I don't mind going to bed early." Kerry did just that, and she was asleep in seconds, it seemed to Angie.

Angie lay awake for a long time, still cold,

still shaking from her experience. Whether it had been real or imagined, she was terrified.

She woke the next morning, sweating from being inside her sleeping bag and covered with several blankets. She felt a bit foolish when she remembered being so scared.

Then even sillier thinking of her bout of jealousy and self-pity. These were her best friends — and her brother. She had never counted Justin as a friend, but maybe she could change her mind. Wouldn't that be funny?

Or maybe — Justin and Paula couldn't have locked her outside, could they? Justin had never been the teasing kind of brother. But under Paula's influence, would he change?

Stop trying to figure it all out, she ordered. She dressed in her swimsuit and a sweatshirt and tiptoed out of the room where Kerry and Paula were still lumps in their beds. She found that she was the only one up. Neither Justin nor Chad was in the kitchen, and no coffee was made. Even though they'd agreed to be on their own for breakfast and lunch, Angie made a pot of coffee. No sense making one cup.

Angie took her coffee out and sat with it on

the beach. The morning was cool, and she wrapped her hands around the warm cup, sipping, letting the liquid warm her inside. Letting the fresh, salt breeze blow away the cobwebs of fear and doubt and confusion.

Gulls hovered overhead, thinking she might have brought them some scraps. Even way out here, they knew that people might mean handouts. A few yards away, one gull rode the waves, bobbing up and down like a bathtub toy. A flock of small birds took no notice of her, but ran up and back, up and back with the tide. When the water was out, they searched the sand for small tidbits of food left exposed. She laughed at the idea of their not wanting to get their feet wet.

When a jolt of energy surged through her whole body from the caffeine, she stood, stripped off her sweatshirt, and waded into the cool water. What a great way to start the day.

Angie was a strong swimmer and thought nothing of wading until a wave knocked her down and then riding out with the same wave into deeper water. With long strokes, she glided and kicked toward a horizon formed by nothing but dark blue ocean.

Common sense caught up with her after a few minutes. She bobbed in the rocking sea and looked back. The old house looked like a sand castle or a child's toy left behind after a beach outing. Not so spooky from this distance.

Did it look haunted? Well, how is a haunted house supposed to look? And daylight helped her sanity to return. She was willing to lay money on Paula locking her out on the balcony. She and Justin had laughed and left after enjoying their joke. And did it matter what was causing the sounds they heard? They could stay outside most of the time, and stay together while they had to be inside.

Turning on her back, she floated, letting the buoyant, salty water hold her effortlessly up. She tried to think of nothing but the warming sun on her face and the cool ocean breeze.

Time meant nothing, but finally her stomach said breakfast would be nice. She flipped over and glanced at the beach to gain her bearings.

Where was the house? Uh-oh, how far had she drifted? She had no idea, but decided it would be smarter to swim to shore and walk back, especially since swimming back meant swimming against the current.

When her knees hit bottom, she stood, swung her hair back over her head, and squeezed out some of the water. She licked her lips and tasted salt, brushed salt from her drying cheeks.

Suddenly, the total isolation she found herself surrounded by made her nervous. Probably because it was so rare. Take two steps in Houston and you run into someone. Now, she couldn't even see the old house in the distance. Not one bird stood on the shoreline.

A billow of clouds drifted across the sun. Angie looked up and shivered. Walking would warm her. She looked back before she started. Nothing, no one. She stared into the dunes. She felt as if she were being watched, but she saw no one. You're doing this to yourself, silly, she thought. She was never going to survive this week if she didn't get control of her nerves and her imagination.

Angie ran for a short distance, but she couldn't keep it up. She slowed to a jog and then had to stop altogether and catch her breath. When she stopped, she heard the footsteps pounding behind her.

Swinging around, she saw a total stranger running toward her. Because she didn't know him, because she was alone, some strange, atavistic terror made her respond without thinking. Someone is chasing you, she thought. Run!

Angie took off again, her feet flying over the cold, packed sand.

Chapter 6

"Wait!" the guy called, running behind her. "I — I didn't mean to frighten you. Stop!"

Angie would have had to stop anyway. Funny how she could swim for miles and yet not run far at all. Her chest ached and her temples throbbed. She bent over to catch her breath.

"Then why did you chase me?" she sputtered, still breathing hard. "You start running after me and expect me not to be scared? Out here where there's no one around for miles?"

"What are you doing here?" He smiled at her, which was certainly enough to make her relax a little.

He had dark brown eyes with thick blond eyebrows that ran together when he smiled. His dirty-blond hair was long and shaggy. He looked a lot like Brad Pitt, and that made her nervous again. Where did this guy come from?

"I could ask you the same. Are you camping up there?" She nodded toward the beach area they'd run away from. "Are you on spring break?"

"Yeah, how'd you guess?" His dark eyes teased her.

"Everyone is. I'm with four friends. We rented a house out here." She wanted him to know she wasn't really alone.

"The old Jamison house?"

"You know it? Are you from Galveston?"

"I used to live on the island. Then we moved to Houston. I miss the ocean, don't you?" He turned and stared out to sea, and the aura of loneliness that surrounded him spread to include her.

She stood beside him and looked at the ocean, matched her breathing to the slow inhaling and exhaling of the tide. That blending with nature's rhythm calmed her immediately.

"I never lived here to miss it. I've always lived in a city. But I do love the ocean. I love to swim out there instead of in a pool. I — I guess I don't like walls, boundaries."

That was a funny thing to tell someone she'd just met. The idea slipped out, though, and she realized it was the truth. She never liked anyone telling her she couldn't do something, go someplace. Her mother couldn't remember that saying no was like waving the proverbial red flag in her face. Like telling her she couldn't come on this trip. Which, by the way, was looking up.

"I saw you swimming," he said. "You seem at home in the water."

"Listen, if you're alone, come up to the house and meet my friends. I haven't had breakfast. I'll scramble us some eggs, and there's coffee unless someone drank it all. If they have, I'll make some more."

"I'd like that. I don't mind being alone, but — well — " He smiled at her again. All the chill she'd felt melted inside her.

"You hear about this place being haunted?" he asked as they came up to the house — which wasn't as far away as she'd thought.

"Yeah, we did, but we decided to risk it. We don't believe in ghosts." We didn't. Until last night. Maybe if he once lived around here . . . But she didn't want to load him down with a lot of questions right off. She didn't want to scare him away, was what she meant. Maybe she'd ask him later if he knew the Jamisons.

"Hey, guys," Angie said, tying her towel around her waist. She had scooped it up, along with her coffee cup, as they'd passed where she'd been sitting earlier. "Look what I found washed up on the beach."

All four sleepyheads were in the kitchen, staring at cups of hot coffee. All four looked surprised at Angie bringing in a guest. But then Kerry grinned at her.

"I forgot to ask your name." Angie felt her face heating up. Names hadn't really mattered until now.

"Val. Val Jensen." Val reached out his hand to Justin, then Chad.

"Like in Kilmer, the movie star?" Paula said. "Or Valentine, like in Saint?" She grinned at Val and shook his hand, too.

He scratched the bit of yellow fuzz on his chin and then smiled the slow smile that was making Angie's toes curl. "No one has ever accused me of being a saint before, so I guess the other guy. He's a movie star? I've hardly ever known anyone with my name. I used to hate it."

"Where've you been? Val Kilmer is only the new Batman," Paula said.

"Here." Angie picked up a cup and started to pour coffee. Someone had made a second pot. "Oh, would you rather have tea?"

"No, coffee would be great," Val said. "I didn't have the energy to start a fire and brew any yet. Smells good." He took the cup from Angie and managed to brush her fingers with his.

Val didn't say a lot once everyone else woke up enough to carry on a conversation, but he smiled and ate a plateful of eggs and toast, and seemed to feel comfortable with her friends. Angie couldn't believe her luck. Someone up there had realized that five was an uneven number.

Justin helped her out. "You're camping? We've got a lot of extra rooms here. You're welcome to take one for the week. If you want company, that is." Justin valued his privacy. He was sensitive to someone wanting to be alone.

Val appeared to think over the offer. "That's really generous of you. But I — I — "

Angie's heart started a fast elevator ride down.

"I'll probably stay put," Val finished his sentence. "But I might come around occasionally. You like fish? I'm good at catching them. We could have a fish fry some night." He smiled at Angie, and she forgave him for wanting to stay in his camp. Good grief, her emotions were on a fast yo-yo ride. "You like to fish, Angie?"

"I — I — "

"Truth or dare." Paula laughed and started washing her dishes.

"Maybe I could learn to like fishing." Angie tiptoed around the truth. She didn't even like eating a fish unless it was cut up and disguised. Shrimp, fine, but a silver body on a plate with an eyeball staring at her was a different matter.

Her friends laughed, knowing her food prejudices but also seeing that she liked Val.

Kerry put her arm around Angie as they prepared to wash dishes together at the sink, where water spurted, stopped, spurted, dribbled, making this chore an adventure at best.

"Do you two have any plans this morning, Angie? The guys want to swim and then go explore the marsh."

"We're going bird watching?" Paula asked.

"Chad and I are." Justin grinned at Paula. "Anyone else is welcome to go along."

"Have you seen the magnificent frigatebird before?" Val asked. "I saw one this morning with his red pouch all puffed up. He's courting." He smiled at Angie. "Only the second one I've ever seen."

"No, are they rare?" Justin said, pulling his notebook over to where he could make some notes. "I'd like to see one."

"You more often get them here after a storm."

It sounded as if Val was willing to go birding. Angie hurried to take a shower and dress, reassured that he wasn't going to disappear if she took her eyes off him.

When she came back outside, Eldon Minor's truck was parked beside the Jeep. Minor was messing around, digging at the corner of the house. Planting something? That seemed strange. Why plant flowers or bushes when the house needed so much work on the inside?

He grinned at Angie and nodded. She didn't speak to him, but walked quickly down to the beach where she could see her friends swimming or playing Frisbee. Brandy liked nothing better than chasing down a plastic disk, so Chad made sure the dog got his exercise.

"Nice dog." Val seemed to appear out of nowhere.

"Oh." Angie jumped. Her nerves were still a bit frazzled from the night's adventures. "Yeah. I think Chad is even crazier about that dog than he is about Kerry. He wants to be a vet." Angie gave Val some time to mention his own interests, but he didn't volunteer any information.

"You go to school in Houston, or down here?" Angie asked.

"Yeah, Houston," Val said.

"I'm a junior at Sam Rayburn High," Angie told him. "I guess I'll go to college in another year, but I have no idea what I want to do. Kerry's going to be a mechanical engineer — I don't know why anyone would want to do that, but she's a super mechanic." She looked at Val in case he wanted to say anything.

"For a girl?" He grinned.

"For a boy or a girl. Justin can't even fix a flat on his bike. He hires me to do it. He wants to be a writer. He'll probably be one of the lucky ones who has best-sellers and then can hire people to do everything for him." She was really babbling, but she couldn't stand the silence between them. She had *thought* this guy liked her, but now she wasn't so sure.

Guys usually liked Angie, but it was after they got to know her. And after she got to know them. Guys merely looked at Kerry and were blown away. Then they'd find out she was taken, of course, but she had that first-glance impact of a model or a movie star.

Angie relied on being fun and friendly and a

good sport to attract the male half of the population. Maybe Val liked someone who wasn't afraid to swim in the ocean alone. Maybe he liked the way she ran. She smiled and felt her face getting hot when she remembered running away from him.

"I think I'd better go now." Val stood up.

"I — weren't you going birding with us?" Angie tried not to sound too disappointed.

"Another time. I left all my gear down there." He jogged away from her, leaving rather abruptly, it seemed to Angie. Had she said something wrong?

She watched Val disappear in the direction of his camp. She hoped he'd come back.

"Who's that boy?" A voice behind her spoke, startling her.

Eldon Minor stood close to her — too close.

"He — " It was none of Minor's business. "Just a friend."

"I thought there was five of you."

"There are. You want more rent because we have a friend?" Angie's voice was sharp. She felt a sudden anger. Was it because of Minor's question or because Val had left?

"I like to know who's hanging around." The old man gripped a shovel in his fist like a weapon.

Angie stood up and moved away from him. "Don't you have work to do?"

"Too much." He shook his head and turned around. "Too much for one man."

Angie watched him walk back to where he had been working.

"I thought you liked Val," Paula said, coming up behind Angie. "Did you decide Eldon Minor was more your type?"

"Paula, *please*. He gives me the willies. But he was asking who Val was. I think he wanted more rent if there were six of us."

"Are there? Six?" Paula smiled and raised her eyebrows.

"Don't I wish." She looked at the empty stretch of sand beyond where the others were playing. "I hope he comes back."

"We don't know anything about him. Except that he's gorgeous. Is that enough?" Paula teased.

"He likes to fish." Angie added up what else they knew. "He ate enough for two. Maybe he's not that good a cook. He likes to camp. He came out here from Houston, too. And — I guess he prefers to be alone most of the time." Angie couldn't keep the misery out of her voice.

Paula patted her shoulder. "He'll be back.

Mark my words. Would I lie to my best friend?"

"Yes." Angie tried to laugh.

"Repeat after me," Paula pushed Angie ahead of her to the house. "He'll be back." She mimicked in an extra-low, Schwarzenegger voice, "I'll be bok."

Angie couldn't stay miserable for long around Paula. She laughed and repeated over and over like a mantra, "He'll be back. He'll be back." Pretty soon she believed it herself.

But when? Today? Please make it today, Val, Angie thought. Like one of your fish, I'm hopelessly hooked.

Chapter 7

Val had taken Angie's mind off haunted houses and ghosts for a short time, but going back upstairs alone to wait for Paula and Kerry to shower reminded her.

All she heard was the soft flutter of the tattered curtains on the windows and the worn draperies on the doors from a breeze that was quickening.

When Kerry came in glistening, her cheeks rosy from the shower, her hair wet and shining, Angie dared ask, "Did you or Paula hear anything this morning, Kerry?"

"Hear what?"

"Jeez, have you forgotten? Did you hear the ghost?"

"No, we didn't hear anything. I think ghosts only come out at night, don't you?" Kerry seemed serious, but also unconcerned, about her observation. She pulled on shorts and a T-shirt and combed her long, wavy hair.

Angie felt slightly angry at Kerry. Was she angry about Kerry's nonchalance or about something else having nothing to do with Kerry at all? Like Val leaving? "I don't think there are any rules for ghost behavior, Kerry. That ghost will come back any time he or she likes."

"I decided not to worry about it." Kerry slid her bare feet into a pair of worn white Keds with a hole in one toe.

"You can do that? Just decide not to worry, and then not?"

"Sure. I'm not going to let a few noises spoil my spring break. Are you?" Kerry smiled at Angie. Then she sat on the bed beside her. "Hey, don't. And I'm glad you met Val. He's really good looking. If I weren't crazy about Chad, I'd give you some competition. Those beautiful brown eyes. That head of hair, like a lion's mane."

"He left." Good thing Kerry *was* crazy about Chad, or Angie wouldn't have a chance to get Val to like her.

"He'll come back. He probably wanted to make sure his camping gear was still on the beach. Maybe he'll even bring it back and move into one of the spare bedrooms so he can be with us all week."

"And maybe Brandy will learn to fly and I'll swim across the ocean like that French guy did." Angie couldn't get her hopes up. She would just be let down.

"What's this about your swimming across the ocean?" Paula bounced into their bedroom. "Not that I'd doubt you could if you put your mind to it, but do you really want to?"

Kerry and Angie laughed, and Angie relaxed a little. She saw that her hands were fists and realized she was hardly breathing. She took in a big pull of salty ocean air and shook both hands to make them stop tensing up. They were on spring break. They were on vacation. She could do anything she set her mind on. She'd set her mind on Val coming back and hanging out with them all week.

To Angie's chagrin, it was Eldon Minor who was hanging out with them all week. She stepped outside to find he'd opened the Jeep's hood and had his head inside, looking over the engine. "Kerry, come here." Angie pointed when Kerry stepped onto the porch.

Immediately Kerry leaped down the steps and headed for her car. Angie followed her.

"May I help you, Mr. Minor?" Kerry said instead of immediately killing the man. She hated anyone even touching her car. "Is there a problem?"

"Some car." Eldon Minor shook his head in wonder. "I'm just looking. Figured you'd dropped another engine in here. The old one would be worn out."

"Yes, I did." Kerry reached for the metal prop for the hood and indicated she was closing the engine back up. "I don't like anyone fooling with my car, Mr. Minor. Hope you don't mind my saying so, but I've spent a lot of time and money restoring this Jeep, and I'm a little protective of it. You understand that, don't you? You're restoring this old house."

The man stared at Kerry. If Kerry had to describe the expression on his face, she'd guess disappointment. "I reckon so. But I was just looking," he said.

"Look, but don't touch." Kerry flashed him her thousand-dollar, thanks to braces, smile. She won over most people that way, especially men and little old ladies.

Eldon wiped his hands on a dirty handkerchief. "Going to the marsh?"

Justin had appeared wearing binoculars. "We thought we would. Any suggestions?"

"Don't you dare ask him to go," Angie whispered and turned away.

"Should we take lunch?" Chad asked as Kerry and Angie returned to the kitchen.

"We're only going a short distance away from the house, Chad. And you just had breakfast. You ate enough for two meals," Kerry reminded him. "At this rate we'll have to go back to Galveston for groceries tomorrow."

"Good idea." Chad grinned and pushed Kerry out the door.

Angie stuck a snack in her bum bag. She was hungry all the time, too, so she sympathised with Chad. Outside, she handed him two chocolate bars and a bag of nuts.

"You carry these, Chad, but I get some cashews later for thinking of your stomach."

Chad took the goodies. "Thanks, Angie. You're all heart."

"And you're all stomach." Kerry punched Chad in the arm and ran. He chased her down the beach until they both collapsed into giggles.

Angie looked back, relieved to see Eldon carrying his ladder. He was watching them, but he wasn't following them to the marsh.

"Let's cut across the dunes here," Justin suggested after they'd walked a short distance. "I'm eager to get into the marsh and see how many birds I can get this trip." Justin wore binoculars around his neck and carried a bird guide for Texas in his hand. He riffled through the pages, studying the pictures. "We should see whimbrels and curlews, maybe some godwits."

"Well, whoop-de-doo." Paula grinned at Justin and flapped her arms. "I can hardly wait." She ducked as he grinned back and took a playful swipe at her.

Angie could see that there was definitely something heating up between her brother and Paula. Who would have thought it possible?

The sand dunes along the edge of the beach were like tiny rolling hills. First they climbed up where strong tides and storms had piled sand higher and higher. Then they dropped down along a flat for a few feet and climbed again.

The marshy area had formed where a stream had meandered on its way down to join the ocean. Since the ocean water often backed up into the marsh, plants that didn't mind salt water or wet feet were the ones that had made a home here.

Angie knew nothing about botany or bird

life, but she enjoyed the idea that a great variety of creatures had made their home near the ocean. They all took turns looking through Justin's or Chad's glasses after Justin spotted another species of bird for them. But mostly Angie just enjoyed breathing the salty, fresh air, walking with her friends, not having to think about assignments or tests or reading another book by the end of the week and reporting on it.

"Hey, look at this, Angie," Justin said, stopping beside her. "I've spotted a rare one. I think it's a resting yellowcap. See what you think." He handed Angie the glasses, took her shoulders, and pointed her in the direction he was staring.

Angie's heart leaped, and not because she'd added a new bird to her life list. The binoculars brought a glimpse of Val Jensen right up to her toes. She almost reached out to see if she could touch him.

"What did I tell you?" Paula whispered. "Let's head in that direction."

"He didn't return," Angie whispered back. "We've come to him."

"Same difference. And he knew we were coming here. He's been waiting for you." Paula ran ahead before Angie could grab her and pull her back. "Hey, Val, see anything good? We just found a curved-bill wahoo."

Val turned and smiled his slow, smoldering smile for Paula, but his eyes continued to move until they lit on Angie. Even she could see the smile reach his dark eyes.

"I didn't see that. Maybe you'd better point it out." He got up from where he sat on a sand dune and walked toward them. He kept walking until he stood beside Angie, and her heart thudded. She imagined it leaping out on a spring, like an animated cartoon of a love story.

To hide her heated cheeks, she turned and walked away from him. She'd look at Val again when she regained her poise.

"Are you a birder?" Val asked Angie as they walked away from the rest of the group.

"No, but I like being outdoors. I guess I could see how exciting it would be to see a rare bird, or even something you hadn't seen before."

"I wish — " Val didn't finish his sentence. His voice trailed off, and he seemed to go someplace else for a little while. Angie finally took his arm to bring him back.

"Anything wrong, Val? Was all your stuff still there?"

"Oh, sure. I don't have anything valuable."

"What were you going to say?" Angie dared ask what thought he'd had that bothered him.

"Oh, maybe I was going to say I wish I'd known you for a long time. I wish we were in the same school. I wish I could keep seeing you when we get back to Houston."

Angie saw nothing in Val's wish to upset her. "Maybe we can. Houston isn't *that* big."

She let it go with that, thinking they could exchange addresses and phone numbers. Not wanting to think about separating at the end of the week. This was only Sunday.

"We have plenty of hamburger meat and hot dogs, Val. Come back to the house with us. We'll cook out on the beach and go for a moonlight swim."

"Hey, I like that idea, Angie. Let's go now. I'm hungry."

"A man I can relate to indubitably." Chad clapped Val on the shoulder. Angie hadn't realized the rest of the birders had caught up with her and Val. "Go, Brandy." He released the dog, who, happy to be free again, took off leaping and barking.

"Val has agreed to help me cook dinner." Angie turned and walked backward for a few steps to make the announcement.

"Hey, that's terrific," Paula said. "Angie is a terrible cook, so we gave her the easy meal. Anyone can flatten ground beef and toss it on the grill. Val, you can unwrap the wieners."

"I can handle that. I can even butter buns." Val caught Angie as she tripped over a piece of driftwood. He leaned down and picked it up. "Let's gather some wood on the way back. We'll have a bonfire."

"Smarter and smarter." Kerry bent to lift a twisted limb herself. "And hey, Val," Kerry said, "if you stay late enough, maybe you can hear our ghost."

Everyone laughed, but Angie wished Kerry hadn't reminded her. She hoped they could live here for five more days without hearing those dreadful sounds of crying again.

Chapter 8

They piled up the wood they'd collected on the beach and then came into the house to change into bathing suits for a swim.

"Going to have a bonfire tonight?" Eldon Minor watched them from two rungs up on a ladder leaning on the house.

Angie felt angry that he'd asked — that he was still there — but Justin answered politely. "Yes, we are. Half the fun of being at the beach is sitting around a bonfire. You going to paint this place someday?"

"Sometimes I think I will. Sometimes I think I'll just let it fall down and start over." He took the two steps down and followed them into the kitchen. "Everything working all right in here? This is old plumbing." Eldon turned water on and off to the kitchen sink.

"Don't talk to him, Justin," Angie whispered. "You're encouraging him to hang around."

The three girls ran upstairs to change. "I think you have two guys sweet on you, Angie. Eldon Minor can't take his eyes off you." Paula laughed and dug in her messy duffel bag.

"Please." Angie took her suit off the balcony where she'd hung it to finish drying. "I don't like that man. I wouldn't put it past him, trying to scare us."

"Why would he do that?" Kerry fluffed her hair in front of the stained and distorted mirror on top of the old dresser.

"He could think scaring us was fun. He lures kids out here, then gets his jollies from playing ghost." Angie sat on her bed and waited for Paula and Kerry.

"I think you've read too many horror novels, Angie." Paula stalked Angie with raised arms and crooked fingers. "Or seen too many Halloween movies." She collapsed in a fit of giggles.

"You wouldn't laugh if he was staring at you all the time." Angie had seen every scary movie that had come out in the last few years. "You remember that movie where a guy this couple had rented to was hiding in the attic watching them? Maybe he's doing that, hiding in the attic."

Kerry sighed. "Angie, please. You'll scare us with your wild imagination. Maybe you should be the writer, not Justin."

With towels, a bag of oils and creams, sunglasses, and romance novels they'd never read, the threesome escaped the house and made a nest on the sand, clean and dry, above the tide line. Angie breathed a lot easier just to be out of that house. She glanced around and imagined all the windows staring at her, the ghost on the upper floor waiting patiently until nighttime.

"Come and swim, Angie," Justin shouted. The guys were already in the water, splashing and yelling across the waves.

"Aren't the waves higher and rougher than they were yesterday?" Paula asked.

"Maybe one of the predicted storms is building up farther out." Kerry stood watching Chad dive into waves as they swelled and crested. "And the tide is coming in, I think."

Val waved at Angie and she waded toward him. As soon as she got close, he dived and swam into deeper water. She caught up and matched him stroke for stroke until they were farther out than even Angie would have gone by herself.

"You're a fantastic swimmer," Val said as he bobbed on the surface and wrung the water out of his long hair, darkened to the color of brass. He swept it back from his eyes. "Are you on the swim team at school?"

"No. I thought about it, but I hated getting up at five A.M. to practice. I would have had to make that my whole life. Are you on any teams?"

Val stared at the horizon. "No," he said and then, finally, "I just like to swim. A storm is coming. I love storms when I'm on the ocean, don't you?"

"Well, not really. Especially when we only have a week of vacation. I hate to have to spend part of it inside."

"You can go out in a storm," Val said casually.

Angie tried to see what Val was looking at. As far as she could see there was nothing, just that flat horizon with dark blue water meeting the lighter blue sky. If she hadn't been with him, she could easily have felt lonely and insignificant.

She couldn't stand the bleakness of the view. "Race you back." She leaped out of the water and swam with a powerful crawl stroke that covered the distance quickly and efficiently.

Suddenly he was beside her and easing ahead. She put out even more effort, but could barely keep up with him. He stood and splashed out onto the beach seconds ahead of her.

Completely winded, she bent double, heaved, and pulled in giant swigs of air. Finally she had enough in her lungs to gasp and laugh, to speak.

"You win. I've met my match."

"I never saw anyone swim like that." Paula had been watching through Justin's binoculars. "I'm impressed with both of you. You must have been a mile or so out."

Justin clapped Angie on the back when she started coughing. "If Val hadn't been out there with you, I'd have worried, Angie. I don't know how Mom expected me to take care of such an idiot."

"We were perfectly safe," Val said, defending Angie. "There's a current but no riptides in this area."

"We worry because the rest of us aren't half fish." Paula grinned and handed the glasses back to Justin.

"Where're Kerry and Chad?" Angie asked.

"They went to look for more driftwood."

"And they wanted to be alone." Justin smiled at Paula. "We do need a lot more wood to keep a fire going for a couple of hours."

"Is that an invitation?" Paula pulled on a T-shirt over her suit. "It's cooling off. We may *need* a fire tonight." She started to walk and then looked back to make sure Justin was following.

"I guess that leaves us to get out the food and start dinner." Angie looked at Val. He was watching Justin and Paula leave. "Val? You want to help with dinner?"

Sometimes Angie felt that Val wasn't with her — or didn't want to be with her. Was that her imagination, or was it her little gremlin who said she wasn't as pretty as Kerry or as much fun as Paula?

"If you want some time alone, I can go make the hamburger patties."

But Val didn't answer her questions. "Paula reminds me of someone — well, she reminds me of my sister." Val finally turned back to Angie. "Not in looks as much as her personality. She's a lot of fun to be around, isn't she?" Val stood up, apparently willing to head for the kitchen.

"Well, yes." And I'm not? Her gremlin again. "She and I have been friends forever — Kerry, too. We went to grade school together. That's the first time you've mentioned your family. You have just the one sister?"

"Yeah. An older sister."

"Are your mom and dad still together?"

"Sure. Aren't yours?" Val looked at her then and smiled.

"Yes, but many of my friends' parents are divorced. Except for Kerry; her parents are still sweethearts. It's funny to watch them together. But Paula's mother and father *should* split up. Her father — well, I think Paula is kind of afraid of him. He's like — like a dictator."

Angie babbled on about parents, families. She felt more comfortable talking, because Val seemed to be paying attention.

"Looks like Mr. Minor is still here, but he moved his truck around back." Val stepped around the house to look. "I'd think if he rented the house to you, he'd stay away for the week."

"I'd feel better if he did." Angie washed her hands and got ready to make hamburger patties. "Surely he doesn't think we're going to invite him to dinner. You want to slice tomatoes and get out all the stuff like mustard and pickles?"

By the time the wood gatherers returned, everything was ready to carry out to the beach.

"Fire's started," Chad said. "It'll be a while before we have coals, though."

"Let's just cook the food over those briquets we bought, and use the bonfire to keep warm." Justin rubbed his arms. "It's getting cold."

"I'm changing to jeans and a sweatshirt." Kerry took off. "Then I'll help," she called back.

Angie changed, too, bringing back a sweatshirt for Val, who had only his T-shirt and jeans over a probably still damp pair of swim trunks. "Here, this is oversized, so it'll fit you." She handed the sweatshirt to Val. She didn't want him to go back to his camp. He might not return.

He slipped it on. "Thanks. That feels good."

The bonfire was roaring by the time the food was ready. No one said much while they dug into roasted corn, burgers, and potato chips and chili dogs for those who had room. Like Chad.

"Oh, I'll never get up." Chad stretched out beside the fire on the blanket Kerry had spread for their dinner table. He put his head in Kerry's lap. Brandy stretched out alongside Chad. Chad lay his hand on Brandy and said, "I could sleep out here."

"The stars are great about two o'clock in the morning." Val spoke for the first time since they started eating.

"That's right. You're sleeping on the beach every night. You sure you don't want to bring your gear into the house?" Chad invited again. "There's a bunch of empty rooms. This must have been a hotel at one time."

"No, the original owner had a bunch of kids." Val put his arm around Angie. She relaxed at last and leaned into his shoulder. "I'll move in if it rains."

Everyone snuggled and stared at the fire as they allowed it to burn low. "I guess no one would want to tell ghost stories?" Paula broke the silence. "Justin is working on one."

"No thanks, Paula," Kerry laughed. "But I think our ghost was a one-time experience."

"Let's hope so." Justin scribbed something in his notebook.

"You brought your notebook out here?" Angie asked, groaning.

"Of course. You never know when I might think of something great, and if I don't get it down, I'll forget it." He read aloud. "The fire burned low, which encouraged the vampire bats to circle closer."

"There aren't vampire bats out here." Angie squealed and laughed at her brother's story idea.

"There could be. They found a cave full of them in Arizona."

The idea broke the romantic mood the three couples had fallen into, and Val chose that moment to stand. "I'd better get back to my camp."

Angie got daring. "I'll walk you a little way." She jumped up and followed Val. "If that's all right with you."

"Sure. Race you." He took off running.

Angie scrambled after him. Fortunately he didn't run far.

Stopping abruptly, Val put his hands on Angie's shoulders and pulled her close. "You're a lot of fun, Angie. I like you."

He smelled of wood smoke and charcoaled hamburgers and fresh ocean air. His face was slightly gritty with leftover salt from their swim.

His lips were warm and soft and tentative. As if he weren't sure she'd want him to kiss her. She would have died if he hadn't. She kissed him back, but before the kiss could deepen, he pulled away. She had to imagine his face in the soft, cool darkness, but it probably held a question. One she didn't want to answer right now. Knowing he cared for her was enough.

" 'Night." He pushed her to arm's length and held on tight for a second.

" 'Night. See you tomorrow." She didn't make it a question, but a fact. Then he'd know she expected him to return.

Val slipped out of her sweatshirt, handed it to her, turned, and jogged away. She stood, listening, the shirt balled in her arms, until she no longer heard the soft thud of his bare feet on wet, packed sand.

The bonfire was still burning when she returned. Chad still lay with his head in Kerry's lap, and Paula and Justin were talking quietly.

Brandy took that moment to snore and kick his legs. Angie giggled and spoke. " 'Night, guys. See you in the morning."

Angie expected to lie awake, thinking about Val. She wanted to do that. But the swim at the end of an active day had tired her, and she fell asleep immediately.

The luminous dials of her travel clock said

2 A.M. when she woke, wondering for a few seconds why.

Music floated around her and through the room. Next came the barely audible sound of voices. And then one of the voices, crying, softly crying. . . .

Chapter 9

Angie lay still, every muscle taut for seconds. "Kerry? Paula?"

No one answered. She called again, louder. Both girls were sound sleepers. "Kerry! Paula, wake up!"

She was fully awake now, so she slipped out of the bed and snapped on the light. The dim overhead bulb allowed her to see that both beds beside her were empty. Where were Kerry and Paula? Had they not come to bed yet? They couldn't be still out on the beach, could they?

The wind had come up and moaned softly around the windows and balcony, flapping the curtains where Angie had left the double doors open. She shivered. Anyone could have come in.

Quickly she pulled on the first sweatshirt

she saw. It was the one Val had worn. It smelled faintly of him, but gave her no comfort. She was alone.

Crying changed to voices, barely audible in the hall. Angie could make out nothing either person was saying. Just that one voice was that of a child, and pleading in tone.

Angie flew down the stairs in seconds. "Paula, Kerry, where are you?"

Kerry and Paula were in the kitchen, laughing and cleaning up the mess from dinner, just as if it were the middle of the day, not 2 A.M..

"Angie, did we wake you up?" Kerry asked, flipping her hair back over her shoulder. "Sorry. We decided we couldn't sleep yet anyway, so we'd try to make a dent in this mess."

"Didn't you hear it?"

"Hear what?" Paula asked.

"The ghost!" Angie collapsed in a chair and started to cry. She couldn't help it. Something about being so scared totally undid her.

Kerry stopped stuffing jars of mayonnaise, mustard, and catsup into the small kitchen fridge. "You heard those sounds again — the music, the crying?"

"Yes, yes. It woke me up, and when you weren't there — "

"Hey, hey, it's okay, Angie." Paula patted

Angie's shoulder. "We're okay. We're right here."

"Let's go upstairs and listen." Kerry wasn't so scared this time. "Maybe we can make out what they're saying."

Paula was willing. "Let's get the guys first. We let them out of clean-up duty, but maybe they aren't asleep yet."

The girls tiptoed back upstairs. They ran to the bedroom the guys had chosen at the end of the hall. Kerry flipped on the light, not caring if she woke them.

"They're not here!" Paula said. For the first time she had a worried look on her face.

"Neither is Brandy. Maybe they took Brandy for a walk." Kerry ran to the balcony and looked over the railing, as if she could see anything in the dark night. Clouds had come in and covered the moon, so the beach was pitch black. Not a shadow moved.

Angie stood beside Kerry and called out in a soft voice, "Justin, Chad. Where are you?"

"So much for protecting the weaker sex," Paula said. "Let's go back into the hall and see if we can hear anything."

"We'd better get our flashlights." Paula stopped at their room, still lit, and gathered all three of their flashlights. Kerry and Angie stood in the hallway and listened.

About a minute had passed when the voices started up again, this time without music. But the voices were still muffled.

"Let's go down the hall on this end and search for another stairway. There has to be one," Angie said, feeling slightly braver.

Angie led the way down the hall, entered the last bedroom on the opposite end of the house, flipped on the light, and walked to the back of the room. She stopped in front of a door.

"Closet," Paula predicted. "Open it."

Angie gripped the cold doorknob and slowly twisted and pulled. The door creaked open. Paula was right, a closet. But near the top of the wall was a grate, like a heating register. And in the ceiling was a panel, like an opening to an attic crawl space.

The two voices they had been hearing floated down through the grate with more clarity. "Caroline, come back," a child called. "Please, come back."

"I can't," a high voice answered. "I can't."

The child began to whimper, then sob.

The three girls listened, clutching arms, huddling together. When the sobbing stopped, soft music started. "Come to your party." The child spoke again, begging, his voice clear over the music.

"I dare you to get a chair and open that panel overhead, Kerry," Paula whispered.

"Why me? I don't want to."

"I will." Angie turned and picked up a small chair that was in the bedroom. The seat was padded, so she'd have to be careful to keep her balance, but she'd be tall enough standing on it.

Paula supported Angie on one side, Kerry on the other, as Angie stepped onto it, curling her bare toes into the softness. "Careful," Kerry said.

Angie flattened both her hands on the square of ceiling that should lift up and out. At first she pushed gently, but the door was stuck. Finally she pushed hard. The door popped up with a thump and a scraping sound.

The voices overhead stopped immediately.

"Shine your light around up there," Paula suggested. "Does it look like a way into the room — if there's one there?"

"No, it's just attic, maybe storage. And it's small."

"Any doors or another panel in the ceiling?"

"I don't see any." Angie tiptoed on the chair, then started to wobble on the soft padding.

"Don't fall. Come on down." Kerry took Angie's hand and helped her.

"If the ghost acts like it did before, it won't speak or cry again now that it's heard us." Paula moved the chair back into the bedroom. "I just realized how tired I am. Let's go to bed."

"Just go to bed?" Angie asked.

"What do you want to do?" Kerry yawned. "Why don't we plan to explore some tomorrow, when it's light. I'm not going to wander around anymore tonight."

As they walked back into the hall, Brandy ran toward them, then stood up on Kerry and licked her face.

Justin and Chad topped the stairs behind the dog. "What's happening, dudes?" Chad asked. "We thought you were asleep."

"Where have you been?" Kerry asked. "You left us here alone, unprotected."

"Three helpless females." Justin laughed. "You hear something again?"

"That child crying." Angie told the story. "He — she — kept calling to Caroline."

"Cool. I'm sorry we missed it." Chad hugged Kerry. "Brandy wanted to go out, and we decided we weren't sleepy. We walked up the beach, thinking we'd find Val's camp."

"Did you?" Angie wanted to know how far away it was.

"No, I got cold," Justin said. "The wind is blowing harder. I think we're in for a storm before long."

"We want to search the whole house tomorrow," Angie said. "We're going to try to find a way into that room overhead — if there is one. It could be all attic."

"Justin and I think we'd better make a run to town to get more food tomorrow." Chad vetoed the search, or postponed it. "Then if it does storm, we can stay inside and play Pictionary or Trivial Pursuit. But we won't starve."

"We'd sure hate for you to starve." Paula put her hands on her hips. "Or have to eat dog food." Chad had brought a huge sack of Kibbles for Brandy. He looked after the dog's stomach, too. "I'm sure we brought plenty of food."

"He might be right, Paula." Kerry voted for town. "And I've been thinking that we forgot to get extra fuel for the lantern we brought. If it storms, the lights could go out. I'd hate to be stranded here at night with no lights."

"We did plan to go shopping." Paula brightened. "We'll have plenty of time to search the house when we get back."

Angie had to give in, and the idea of going to the city, the idea of getting out of this house for a day, *was* appealing.

"Okay, let's get some sleep. At this rate we won't wake up till noon." Angie started to their bedroom, but then she had an idea. "I'll be there in a minute. I just have to check something."

Outside, she shone her flashlight to make a path around the front of the house and toward the driveway in back. It took only a second to find out what she wanted to know. The beam of transparent yellow spotted Eldon Minor's old truck, still parked where he'd left it earlier.

Eldon was here, someplace in the old house. Maybe in the attic, pretending to be a child.

Chapter 10

Angie was too tired to let what they'd heard keep her awake. When she woke midmorning, she was glad to see sunlight streaming into their room and hear only the hush of the waves as they washed up and back. As she lay there, lulled into a meditative state, a gull screeched, bringing her fully awake again.

"Hey," she said, sitting up. "Let's get out of here for the day. Anybody game?"

Paula and Kerry came alive reluctantly. No one had slept *enough*, but they didn't come here to sleep.

Paula grinned, remembering. "I was born to shop. Let's go."

They grabbed quick wake-up showers and cups of coffee and decided to eat breakfast and lunch at the same time once they got to the city. Except for Chad. He munched a breakfast bar as he did a fast inventory of groceries they had left.

"What about Val?" Angie asked. "Shall we try to find him? He'd probably like to go."

"You mean you'd like him to go, right?" Paula grinned.

Angie smiled. Then her smile spread wider and into a grin as Val walked in. "Did I hear my name taken in vain?"

"Val, you did." Angie hugged him, not caring what he or anyone else thought. "We're getting ready to go into the city for the day. We want you to come with us."

"We're going shopping, and then we'll get lunch, and probably dinner, before we return. We've had enough of our own cooking."

Val stared at his bare toes, then squatted down and petted Brandy, who rubbed against him. "You taking Brandy?"

"Sure," Chad answered. "Where I go, Brandy goes."

"He's going to be ring bearer when they get married," Paula teased.

"I'd better stay here. I was going fishing this morning." Val looked at Angie. She couldn't read his eyes. Was he wanting her to beg, or did he really not want to go?

"You can go fishing tomorrow morning,"

Paula said. "I like my fish fresh. We need our pizza fix tonight."

"Well, I'll eat the ones I catch today and catch some more tomorrow. I'm good at fishing." Val turned and walked back toward the beach.

"I think he doesn't have much money." Angie turned to Kerry and the others. "Is everyone willing to treat? We'll buy his dinner tonight and he'll bring fish tomorrow night." She started thinking of ways to make this okay with Val.

"Sure. I'm loaded now that we got this mansion cheap." Chad whistled to Brandy to get into the Jeep.

Angie ran after Val. "Val wait. I don't want to embarrass you, but if you're not going because you're short on money, we'll treat. And you can treat with the fish."

Val blushed slightly, and he avoided Angie's eyes. "I am short on money. You guessed right. But I'd really rather go fishing, Angie. You and your friends — you're all so close, and — I — "

"Everyone likes you, Val."

Angie stalled to give Val time to decide. Then she looked at him again. "Maybe I could stay here and go fishing with you. I'm inviting myself, but — " She was torn. She wanted to go into Galveston and shop and eat, but she wanted to be with Val. She really wanted him to go with them.

"I want you to go with us." She might as well be truthful.

"Thanks, Angie. I'd enjoy going, but I think I need the day to myself. I'll stay here. I'll come back same time tomorrow, and you can go fishing with me then. If you don't mind a leaky boat. There's one in the boathouse here. I think it will float with some encouragement."

"You're going fishing in a leaky boat?" Now Angie had something else to worry about.

"Not that leaky. And I might be able to fix it, depending on what else I find on the shelves in there."

"Did you ask Eldon Minor if it was all right to use a boat?"

"Sure. He doesn't care."

He probably didn't care. And he was gone this morning anyway. Angie had made a point of looking. She hadn't heard his truck start, but then she'd slept like the dead.

Angie hugged Val again, and this time he hugged back. "Be careful."

"I will." He gave her that slow grin that made her shiver. "Eat some pizza for me. No anchovies." He turned and jogged away.

Angie watched him for a few seconds and then shrugged. She ran to get into the Jeep. Everyone was waiting for her.

"No luck?" Paula asked, putting her arm around Angie for solace.

"No. He seems to want to be alone. I practically asked him if I could stay here with him and go fishing."

"Is that what you wanted to do?" Kerry turned and smiled at Angie.

"No, I wanted to go to town. But I wanted him to go along." She shrugged again. She looked out the window and hoped no one saw the tears form in her eyes.

"He's one of those people who likes to be alone, Angie." Paula hugged her. "A romantic mystery man."

The Jeep bounced and tilted as Chad maneuvered around the worst of the ruts on the deserted beach road. He munched another breakfast bar at the same time.

Kerry studied a book and map they'd gotten from AAA before they'd left. "Did you know Galveston used to be called Campeachy, and that it was the biggest city in Texas?"

"Campeachy? No kidding," Justin said. "When was that?"

"Before 1900. The hurricane that year totally destroyed it. The city never recovered, except that they've restored a lot of the old city now, and they have festivals all year round."

"We don't have to do a tour, do we?" Paula grimaced. "Like study the history and all that?"

"It would be — "

Angie interrupted Justin. He was always in favor of learning something. "You know us better than that. This is strictly a shopping, eating, stocking-up trip. Then back to the beach. I wish I'd had time for a swim this morning."

"With Val." Paula might be sympathetic, but she also liked to tease.

The teasing and laughing and squealing and giggling never stopped as they spent the day eating super subs and Cokes, buying great T-shirts, eating homemade, double-dip chocolate almond fudge ice cream, then admiring a little of the architecture of the old buildings as they rode the trolley around town.

Angie bought herself a coffee mug painted with tropical fish and then decided on one for Val decorated with an aqua-green background. It wasn't a personal gift, but maybe he'd like it. Maybe he'd realize it said she had thought of him off and on all day. Since she had. She missed him. She hoped he missed her.

On the way back, they stopped at the same small store where they'd gotten supplies the first night. Myra Adams recognized them. "Hello. How are you getting along out there in the haunted house?"

Angie looked at Paula and Kerry. Should they tell Mrs. Adams the place really *was* haunted?

Kerry made the decision. "We love it. Except that Mr. Minor is out there all the time. I guess he warned us."

"Eldon is harmless," Mrs. Adams said as she packed grocery sacks. "He looks a little strange, and I guess you heard he's an ex-con. But he came back here and made a pretty good life for himself. To tell the truth, I think he's lonely."

Angie looked at the shocked expessions on her friends' faces and knew hers probably registered the same emotion. Eldon Minor had been in prison?

"What was he in prison for?" she asked.

"An accident really. Fight in a bar in town. He got off with manslaughter and a light sentence. He was young and had never been in trouble before." Myra Adams's voice trailed off, mumbling something about justice as she totaled their bill.

Back in the car, Angie said sarcastically, "That makes me feel a lot better. I mean, that it was an accident that Eldon Minor killed someone. We're not living around a *real* murderer."

"She said he was harmless," Justin reminded Angie.

"In her opinion. A harmless murderer." Angie took a breath. "I'm going to ask him to leave next time he comes out, leave us alone the rest of the week. Will you guys back me up?"

"Sure," Kerry agreed. "He can take a few days off. He hasn't been making any progress that I can see anyway."

Paula grimaced. "I wish we could lock the doors at night. 'Course, he'd have a key."

Myra recommended what looked like a small tavern near her store for the best pizza on the island. Even Chad groaned as they started home after devouring two huge everything-on-it pies. "I may not be hungry again for a couple of days."

"Or at least a couple of hours." Angie watched the sun set, spreading a rosy glow over the ocean before dropping into the water. She imagined the sizzle as the fiery ball entered the navy-blue depths.

Despite what they'd learned about their landlord, a full stomach, the warm car, and last night's lack of rest lulled Angie to sleep. Her eyes kept closing; then she'd be jerked awake by Chad hitting a bigger than usual bump.

Her eyes flew open, though, and she came to total alert when they got close enough to see the house.

"Look," almost everyone said at once.

"The house — it's — "

"Every light in the place must be on."

"Eldon's back. There's his truck right in front with both doors hanging open."

"I don't see him. What in the world is going on?"

"Do we really want to know?" Angie had a sinking feeling.

Chapter 11

The front door to the house was wide open. Justin and Chad led the way in, and, sticking close together, the five soon searched the bottom floor of the old house.

Music floated down to them from above.

"Let's see if we can find another way to that upstairs room," Angie suggested.

"I vote we search the servants' quarters first," Justin said. "We'll do this logically."

"There's nothing logical about a ghost." Paula took his arm. "But that might be a good idea."

Angie had to go along, since she didn't want to be alone.

Nothing seemed out of place in the kitchen except that the door leading upstairs to the probable servants' quarters stood open. Angie looked at her friends and then led the way up the narrow staircase.

All the lights were on in the hall and small bedrooms, but no one was there. The music was louder, and now the tune was familiar. "The music is more modern now," Kerry said. "Does that mean anything?"

"Who knows?" Chad took her hand.

"Look, guys. We never saw this before." Angie pointed as they descended to the kitchen. "More stairs leading down; there must be a basement."

Before anyone could say "don't go there," Angie kept stepping down. A musty smell surrounded her, and it was much cooler.

Bare lightbulbs on pull strings lit up the cellar room. The area seemed to be used for storage. Along one wall were shelves with ancient cans of paint, flowerpots, fertilizer, and rat poison. An old mattress lay in one corner, some of the stuffing pulled out and spread around. In one corner leaned some tools — shovels caked with dirt, a big broom, rakes, a pitchfork.

"Should we turn off the lights as we leave?" Kerry asked.

"I guess so." Justin pulled one off. "Why are they all on?"

"If we knew that, maybe we'd know what was happening here." Angie pulled the last string, leaving them in light only from the stairs. They practically ran over each other getting out.

Justin tiptoed quietly upstairs and turned off those lights, too, as everyone waited for him.

Angie took a deep breath. "Okay, let's look on the second floor. And this time, guys, we're going to find a way into that top floor. There has to be some passageway."

"A secret passageway?" Paula said. "Are we in a Nancy Drew story?"

"No, Hardy boys." Justin grinned and squeezed her arm.

Everyone was acting really brave, as if they did this all the time, searched old, haunted houses, but Angie knew her friends were probably as jittery as she was. They just didn't want to admit it. There was strength in numbers, though, so they moved almost as one body with ten legs.

First they went to the guys' room. Lights on but nothing amiss. Then to the other end of the hall.

Angie was the first to enter their bedroom. She gasped and held her hand to her chest. "It's — it's — "

"Eldon Minor," Justin finished her sentence, kneeling on the floor beside the man sprawled in front of the open double doors. He held his hand to Minor's neck. "He's alive."

Angie let out the breath she'd been holding. As much as she disliked the man, she didn't want him to be dead on her floor. "What is he doing here? Who hit him?"

"How should I know?" Justin was as rattled as Angie had ever seen him. Carefully he looked at the matted blood where Minor had been hit over the head.

Everyone stood watching, wondering what to do, when Eldon groaned. Slowly he regained consciousness; even more slowly, he sat up and cradled his head in one hand.

"What happened, Mr. Minor?" Justin asked. "Who hit you?"

"And why was every light in the house on?" Angie added.

"What are you doing in our room?" Kerry had her own question. No one considered that Eldon Minor couldn't answer four questions at once.

Brandy whined, and Chad held him back to keep him from offering his brand of sympathy to the man still blinking his eyes, trying to remember.

"I — I heard that music, and I could see that none of you was in the house. I came in, looking around. I turned on all the lights while I was searching. I turned around to leave, when bang, the lights went out — my lights." He touched his head wound and groaned again.

For the first time Angie looked around. The room had been turned upside down. Their clothes were dumped on the beds and floor.

"Did you make this mess, Mr. Minor?" Angie asked, getting angry. "Why did you go through all our things?"

"I didn't do that. Honest, I didn't. I didn't have much time to look, to notice, but I don't remember this mess being here when I came in." Minor tried to stand up. Chad and Justin rushed to help him.

As if he noticed the music for the first time, Eldon Minor looked up at the ceiling. "Myra was right," he whispered.

"Do you know how to get up there?" Justin asked.

"Nope. Hadn't gotten around to it. Decided to repair the outside of the house first. Now I won't look. You couldn't pay me enough to live out here." Eldon looked like a startled rabbit ready to bolt. "This place *is* haunted. I'm leaving. Maybe you should leave, too. I'll refund some of your money — all your money." Eldon, holding his head, started for the bedroom door.

As Eldon left, the music stopped. The house was silent, deadly silent. Not a creak, a crack, a moan.

Paula broke the silence. "If he'll leave and promise to stay away, I don't mind staying. What's a little night music?"

Angie agreed about staying without Eldon Minor there, but the "ghost" was another matter. "I say let's find out what's going on right now, tonight. I don't want to stay here and be afraid."

"You won't be afraid if we find it?" Kerry asked, still clutching Chad's arm, still huddling close to him.

"Depends on what we find. Does a ghost tune in to one of today's radio stations? A ghost is from the past. That song we heard earlier is one of today's top hits."

Angie's reasoning left her less fearful than she had been before. If everyone would go with her, she was willing to search all night.

"Is everyone game?" she asked. "I'm not going alone."

Chad looked at Kerry. Paula looked at Justin, then Angie. They all nodded at the same time.

"Then come on. Let's go play ghostbusters." Angie headed out the bedroom door into the hall and toward the closet with the panel in the ceiling.

Chapter 12

Justin got the bedroom chair, put it in the closet, and pushed up the panel in the ceiling, even though Angie told him there was nothing there. He even lifted himself into the crawl space and looked around.

"Careful, Justin," Paula called. "We don't want you crashing through the ceiling."

While Paula helped Justin step down, Angie knocked on the back wall of the closet. "Listen, guys, it sounds hollow." She continued her tap, tap, tap from one side to the other. There was a *bonk*, *bonk*, *bonk*, then a *thud* when she hit a wall that was more solid.

Following some intuition, as if she did this every day, she ran her fingers over the wall, looking for any place that wasn't smooth.

"Here! Feel this." She ran her fingers vertically along a slight indentation. "I think there was once a door here, but someone wallpapered it over."

Angie dug her fingernails into a crack until she got the paper to rip. Dust and the musty smell of rotting paper filled her nostrils. She tried to hold back a sneeze, but made a muffled *choo* sound in her fist.

"Quiet," Chad whispered.

"If anyone's in there, they've heard us by now." Justin slid fingers alongside Angie's to the top of the wall.

"Did we pay a damage deposit?" Kerry said, with a nervous giggle. "Are you going to tear into that wall?"

Now Angie had a curl of paper tearing off along the seam. With their flashlights focused on the wall, it took only seconds to see there was a door behind the ancient wallpaper.

Everyone joined in the ripping and tearing, filling the small space with a fine, powdery dust. Angie's eyes watered, and she blinked to clear them. She sneezed twice, no longer trying to be quiet. In minutes they exposed a door.

"I'm not going in first." Paula stepped back into the bedroom, brushing the dust from her shirt and shorts.

"I will if you're all right behind me." Angie

pushed the door — it had no knob — and the hinges creaked. The bottom of the door grated against the bare floor.

They shone light in as far as possible before Angie took that first step.

"It's a short flight of stairs," Angie said as she started up.

The steps creaked and popped as if no one had used them for years. At the top of the stairs, a door opened easily, making no sound.

"I'm going in," she whispered, making sure her four friends were behind her. A few steps in, she swung around and searched the wall for a light switch.

The powerful beam of her flashlight glanced off the big windows that faced the ocean, momentarily blinding her. She moved in that direction and kept the beam searching.

"There, there's a light switch. I'm going to try it." She left the others and tiptoed to the far side of the big room. As she passed the windows a flimsy curtain billowed out and brushed her face softly. She gasped.

"What is it?" Kerry heard the sound.

"Nothing. A curtain. I didn't expect the window to be open." She clawed away the sheer cloth and kept walking until her fingers grasped the small switch. She flicked it up.

Dim light flooded the room from an overhead, chandelier-type fixture.

"The room has been decorated," Paula whispered.

"A long time ago," Justin added. "These are decorations from the last party someone had here."

Streamers of crepe paper, faded from red to a pale pink, were draped along the top of the walls. Twisted strands of pink and white ran from the corners of the room and tied onto the chandelier.

A number of chairs waited for party guests around the room or huddled in clusters as if ready for gossiping, giggling people, waiting to dance. The floor was waxed and polished to a high shine so partners could waltz and spin.

"It's kind of sad, isn't it?" Angie said, when her eyes had taken in all the room. She shivered, remembering the crying. And the voices . . . "One last party in the old house," she said quickly, "and then people moved away. They didn't even bother to take down the decorations."

Chad hadn't tried to keep Brandy from exploring with them. Now the dog ran from corner to corner, from chair to chair, his claws clicking on the wooden floor. Suddenly the dog stopped, turned back to a spot he'd passed. He sniffed again, then whined.

"What is it, Brandy?" Chad hurried over to see what the dog had found. "Look, guys, it's a radio-tape player."

"It's *my* CD player." Kerry leaned over and grabbed it up. "Someone took it out of my room and brought it up here. Must have been earlier tonight. I hadn't missed it."

"The clock has a timer, doesn't it?" Chad said. "So you can program it to come on in the morning and wake you up. I'll bet Eldon Minor set it to blast on about the time we came home."

"Then went downstairs again and knocked himself out?" Justin couldn't buy into what Chad was suggesting.

"Someone brought it up here. Who else — " Kerry stopped, mid-sentence. "Val was here; I mean, he didn't go to town with us."

"You think Val stole your radio, brought it up here and turned it on, then knocked out Eldon Minor?" Angie said. "Yeah, right. Why would Val do that?"

"He's heard us talk about our ghost." Justin fingered some paper flowers tied to the top of one of the chairs. "Maybe he thought it would be a great joke to turn the music on just as we got home. Minor surprised him because he usually doesn't come into the house."

"Val wouldn't hit Eldon over the head because he spoiled a joke," Angie said.

"Could have been two separate incidents." Justin was still trying to make sense of the evidence they had. "Val got bored, decided to play a trick on us. He put the radio up here and then left. Minor came in the house first, surprising a burglar, who knocked him out."

"Someone came out here to steal something?" Paula laughed without much enthusiasm. "How about Myra Adams, or someone who was in the convenience store and heard us talking about being out here all week. Someone could have seen us going to town and figured they'd come out here and see if we had anything valuable."

"Maybe Myra and Eldon are in cahoots. She tells people about this place when they're desperate for a rental. Then, because it's really remote, she and Eldon can rob them after they move in." Justin was into one of his stories, thinking of all sorts of mystery and intrigue.

Kerry shook her head. "I think we're trying to make sense of something impossible to figure out. Let's get out of this room. I'm getting really creepy vibes from being up here."

"In the phantom ballroom," Paula said in a quivery voice. She was ready to make wisecracks again.

"It *was* a great party room, wasn't it?" Angie tried to imagine what the room had been like when the house was built.

Everyone had ignored Brandy until he whined again. He had found a dresser or cupboard of darkly stained wood pulled out a ways from the wall. The dog stood behind it, and they could see only his tail wagging furiously.

"Atta boy, Brandy." Chad ran to him. "He's found another door."

"The other door?" Kerry asked.

"That's right." Justin hurried over to the large piece of furniture. "Whoever brought the radio up here couldn't have come in the way we came in."

The door Brandy discovered opened into what proved to be the end of the third-floor hall, but they had to push aside another big piece of furniture to get out.

Kerry leaned against the wall. "I just realized how tired I am, guys. Surely we've scared away whoever was here. Let's turn in."

"So we're going to stay here tonight?" Paula asked.

"I'm not driving back to town, and where else would we stay?" Kerry led them down the two flights of stairs to the kitchen.

"I'll make some cocoa." Angie filled the tea kettle and placed it on the stove, lighting the gas with a *whoomp*. "There are five of us. It's not like we're out here alone," she went on. She was over her fright, and certainly too tired to go anyplace except to bed. "If we're nervous about staying here, we'll pack and leave tomorrow."

"That's a plan." Justin collapsed in a chair. "I'm not scared. Is anyone?"

They exchanged glances and no one would admit it if he or she was scared to stay one more night in the old house.

"I'd like to see that ballroom by daylight." Angie filled five cups with cocoa powder, and when the kettle whistled, she poured steaming water into each.

After a few sips of chocolate, Justin said, "Why didn't Eldon Minor go to town and get the police? Someone assaulted him. Wouldn't he report it?"

"Not if he faked it." Chad rubbed Brandy's

ears. "Not if he meant to go through all our things and get out of here before we got back. We got back early and surprised him."

"But he had a bump on his head," Kerry argued. "He didn't knock himself out for an alibi."

Angie was tired of trying to make sense of the evening's events. She cupped both hands around her mug, her mind drifting to focus on Val. She had halfway expected him to be at the house to greet them, maybe holding up his string of fish, asking to put them in the fridge for tomorrow.

She realized that she was disappointed that he wasn't there. Her mind had been dramatically distracted by finding Eldon and then looking for and finding the way into the ballroom. Now that she had time to think, though, Val was all she wanted to think about.

Everyone would sleep late. She was going to get up early. She was going to look for Val's camp until she found it, and him. He might not like her invading his privacy, but she couldn't sit and wait for him to come to her. Her heart ached with loneliness, and whether he had meant to be or not, he was the cause of that emotion. She would even swallow her pride and say, "I missed you. I had to find you, to see you again."

She crawled into bed with that plan. Find Val. Hold him tight until he admitted he missed her, too.

Chapter 13

Angie woke, surprisingly rested, after only a few hours of sleep. She remembered nothing after falling into bed. Perhaps exploring the ballroom and finding nothing — no one — there had taken away some of the fear she'd felt after hearing the voices and music several times.

The unknown was what was frightening. The musty, still-decorated ballroom was only sad, as if the family living here last had thrown one last farewell party before they moved. The party had faded to a memory for them. Angie felt as if she had seen that memory last night, and this morning she felt nothing but sadness. And, of course, loneliness.

She couldn't remember ever feeling this empty, hollow core. Why did she feel it so intensely this week?

She knew the answer to her question. She admitted it while she waited for a pot of coffee to drip.

She was used to seeing Kerry and Chad together. They had been a couple for so long, she thought nothing of it. And she still had had Paula. But now one couple had become two. And she had met Val. For the first time she cared deeply about someone. The caring had happened so fast. What was it about him that touched her heart? That he, too, was alone? That he retreated so easily deep into a space inside himself that was so intense she could almost feel his loneliness?

Suddenly she knew she must find him.

She scribbled a note: *Gone to look for Val.* She slipped out the front door before anyone else was awake.

On the beach, she looked both ways. There was no sign of human life for as far as she could see in either direction. The birds were there, of course. They performed their morning ritual of searching for food on the beach or from the air.

Angie smiled and continued to walk. A brilliant sun rose on the eastern horizon, glancing off waves and dunes, but scarcely warming the morning. To the west, huge billows of clouds, blue tinged on the bottom, gray, then white with a hint of yellow, built, probably forecasting the rainy end to the week they had been promised.

Angie stared in the direction she walked and wondered how far she'd already come with no hint of a camp, no clue that anyone was living out here. She turned and stared out to sea, feeling even more lonely than when she'd left the house. Maybe some exercise would lift her mood. She pulled her sweatshirt over her head.

A slight breeze raised tiny bumps on her arms and legs and lifted the hairs on the back of her neck. She waded until the waves lapped at the bottom of her swimsuit; then she took a breath and dived into the next swell of greenish-blue water.

With long, strong strokes, she glided along the surface of the ocean with ease. She swam as far out as she had the first morning she was here, buoyant and energized by the salty sea. Then she floated, knowing the current was taking her in the direction she wanted to go. Val had found her out here once. Maybe she couldn't find him. She'd have to wait until he found her.

But when the sun had risen halfway up the

bowl of faded blue sky, she knew she'd better go back to the house. She didn't want to worry anyone. She fought back her own worry.

Had Val gone out yesterday in the leaky rowboat as he'd planned? Had he returned? How long would she have to wait to find out? With a rush of impatience and disappointment, Angie headed for shore.

By the time she had walked all the way back to the house, everyone was awake and hanging out on the beach. Paula waved as soon as she spotted Angie.

"Angie. Here she is, Justin." Paula turned back and shouted to Justin, who had apparently returned to the house for the tray he was carrying.

Angie realized she was starving and picked up her pace. She collapsed on Paula's towel.

"Where have you been, Angie? I was getting worried." Justin frowned at her.

"I left a note. I was looking for Val."

"All this time? Did you find him?" Justin should have been able to see that she hadn't.

"No, and I'm worried. He said he was taking out that old rowboat yesterday." Angie reached for a breakfast bar, tore the wrapper off, and crunched a bite.

"Did you check to see if the boat was back in the boat house?"

"No, but I will right now." Angie scrambled to her feet. She should have checked there first. Maybe Val hadn't taken the boat out, and she was worrying for nothing.

Justin and Paula followed Angie to where the leaning metal shed perched above the high-tide line. Angie pulled open the screeching door and peered inside. She blinked a few times to adjust to the dim interior.

"No rowboat," she said, feeling some disappointment. "Val did take it."

"He could have beached it way down on the shore where he was camping." Paula stepped inside the shed.

"I walked a long way." Angie followed Paula, as did Justin.

He looked around. "It seems strange that whoever lived here last left all this stuff."

"Maybe they moved to the city." Paula had a ready answer. "Maybe they sold everything to Eldon along with the house."

"I guess so," Justin said reluctantly.

The inside of the shed was a disorderly mess, with nets, oars, lanterns, a couple of rotting life jackets. Tools were scattered on a counter, a few items hung on a pegboard wall, and fishing rods leaned in a corner. Just the ordinary stuff you'd collect living on the ocean, playing, fishing.

But one shelf stood out from the rest. In a very orderly fashion, shells and a few bird skulls were displayed. Why would someone leave what was clearly a carefully gathered collection behind?

Again, as when she stood in the decorated ballroom, Angie had the idea that she was sharing someone's memory.

As they watched the storm slowly build, they knew they'd better enjoy this sunny day. It might be the last for the week if bad weather hung around for a couple of days.

Angie made tuna sandwiches and brought them down to where they'd settled with their towels and lotions and books to look at but hardly to read. Kerry carried a pitcher of iced tea.

"Still worried about Val?"

"Of course." Angie confessed her real fear. "Maybe he won't come back. Maybe for some reason he's already gone back to Houston."

"Maybe not, oh, ye of little faith." Kerry hugged Angie, but returned to her towel beside Chad and Brandy.

About three o'clock, after Angie had drifted into a light sleep, she heard his voice and thought for a moment she was dreaming.

"Ahoy the shore. Anyone getting hungry?"

She sat up to see Val pulling the old rowboat up onto the packed wet sand. Her entire body flooded with relief, and she realized just how worried she had been.

"Have you been out there fishing since yesterday?" she asked.

"Of course not. I brought one load of fish in yesterday, ate them, then had to go for a second run. I promised you dinner, didn't I?" He held up a string of silver-colored fish, each one weighing several pounds.

Val acted as if being gone for about thirty-six hours was no big deal. He offered no apology, no explanation — and, of course, he owed them none. But most people would have said where they'd been. He'd obviously been in the sun. His skin had changed quickly from pale pink to a healthy, golden brown. His shoulders were slightly red from the day's exposure, but he had the kind of skin that darkens easily.

Angie's relief started to turn to anger, but she stopped herself. Being mad would only spoil the evening, too.

"I'll find some wood." She jumped up.

"I need some helping cleaning these." Val smiled at her.

"I'll help Angie gather wood for a fire." Paula hurried toward the dunes.

"Me, too." Kerry joined Angie and Paula as the three guys laughed. Brandy bounced and barked at the string of fish.

"Down, boy," Chad commanded.

Angie's spirits had instantly risen about a hundred percent. The evening ahead was going to make up for all the worrying she had done about Val — for nothing.

Chapter 14

"Run," shouted Angie, grabbing her plate, loaded with fish, coleslaw, and garlic bread toasted on a stick over the open fire.

No one protested or disobeyed her orders, since big drops of rain splattered and hissed in the coals of their fire. The huge storm clouds that had been gathering all day had turned to navy and charcoal gray in the last hour. Lightning bolts provided beach-party fireworks in the western sky.

Brandy, afraid of the thunder, had long since disappeared and was probably under Chad's bed. He might have been the smartest of them all. But they had to hold on until the fish were all cooked to a flaky pink. As it was, they left their baked potatoes still smoldering in the smoking coals.

There was a cozy feeling to crowding over

the kitchen table, dry and quickly easing growling stomachs, while rain poured and wind howled.

"Think the windows will break out?" Kerry asked, looking at the bashing the glass panes were taking from the slanting attack of water.

"I'm sure this isn't the first storm they've stood up to." Chad pulled the long spine with bony ribs from the middle of his fish. "This is the best fish I ever ate. Thanks, Val."

Val mumbled and kept his eyes on his plate. He seemed half starved.

"Is that the first meal you've had today?" Angie teased.

"I think so." He looked up long enough to catch her eyes and smile, then returned to eating.

"You think so?" Chad laughed. "Some people pay attention to stomachs, some don't."

"And we know what camp you're in, Chad," Paula said. "That of the stomach tenders."

"Better than tending to other people's business." Chad shoveled in a heaping forkful of coleslaw.

"I love other people's business." Paula licked her fingers. "What did you do all day yesterday, Val?"

Angie was glad Paula asked for her.

"Oh, fished, bailed water out of the boat, and just messed around. I lose track of time easily." Val didn't seem offended by Paula's nosiness. Of course, he did evade the question somewhat. How can a person spend almost two days messing around?

"I lose track of time when I'm writing." Justin reached for the dish of slaw.

"How much writing have you gotten done this week?" Angie teased, looking at Paula, who grinned.

She rarely saw her brother blush, but the fact that he did now made her like him even better. She was enjoying her brother's company. Who would have ever thought? She grinned back at Paula, who looked like the proverbial cat who'd caught the canary.

"I've gotten a lot of ideas." Justin couldn't let Angie win entirely.

He had left himself open for another wisecrack from Angie, but he escaped her barb when an especially loud thunderclap shook the old house.

"Wow, that was close." Chad stood up. "I'd better check on Brandy. He's probably having a heart attack by now."

Paula and Kerry scraped fish bones from near-empty plates and stacked dishes for washing. "We'll clean up, Val. You caught the fish. Why don't you and Angie take your drinks and find someplace cozy to watch the storm. It doesn't look as if the rain is going to stop anytime soon."

Bless you, Kerry, Angie thought. Before Val could protest, Angie stood and headed for the living room.

"Let's build a fire," Angie suggested, knowing Val might feel awkward. "I never expected to be cold down here this time of year, but the storm sure lowered the temperature."

Val got to work wadding paper and stacking kindling in the big, old fireplace without saying a word. He was the quietest Angie had seen him since they'd met.

The fire crackled and popped, and they added a few larger logs. "I looked for you this morning," Angie admitted.

"I — sometimes I lose track of time."

"You already said that."

"I — I'm sorry if you were disappointed." He stared at the flames.

Angie placed her hand on Val's arm. "It's all right, Val. I didn't expect you to sit around here waiting for me to come back from town."

He smiled at her and then stared into the fire again.

"Is anything bothering you, Val?" Angie asked.

"I don't think so. Do I look bothered?"

Angie was relieved when her friends tumbled into the room before she could think of an answer. She hadn't known Val long enough to recognize the difference between bothered and quiet or pensive.

"Who's for Pictionary?" Paula plopped down on the floor beside the low coffee table and unfolded the game.

"I'll play if I don't have to be your partner." Kerry sat beside Paula but patted the floor beside her for a returning Chad. "How's Brandy?"

"Miserable. But he won't come out from under the bed, so he'll have to suffer alone." Chad helped pass out pencils and pads of paper.

"Any caring owner would stay under there with him." Paula motioned to Angie and Val to join them.

"He's supposed to be my best friend, not the other way around. And there's too much dust under these beds." Chad proved it by sneezing three times in a row.

"I — I don't know how to play this game." Val stood, didn't take a seat in the circle.

Angie took his hand and tugged him around to the other side of the table. "Well, it's incredibly difficult to learn, but I guess I'll take you for my partner and help you."

"First, can you draw stick figures?" Paula gave Val an extremely serious scowl.

"Stick figures?" The look of confusion on Val's face made everyone laugh, and Angie felt him stiffen beside her.

"Val, we're just kidding," Angie said quickly. "A six-year-old could play this game."

They didn't think it possible but the storm grew worse. Warm and dry, they were aware of the thunder boomers and the downpour, but they chose to enjoy the noise and their game. They laughed so much, no one was too serious about winning or losing.

"I quit," Chad said after getting *peculiar* as the word he had to draw. "I've had the hardest words all evening. I'm going to join Brandy."

Paula picked up the game and looked at Val. "Val, tonight, we insist. You're staying overnight. There's a perfectly empty bedroom in the male wing of this dormitory."

"I guess you're right. I'd hate to be in a sleeping bag on the beach right now." Val stepped over to look out the big picture window that would have an ocean view by day.

Angie looked at him for a minute, then decided to leave him alone. Maybe he didn't have a lot of experience with girls.

In their room, Paula expressed her sympathy. "He may be the best-looking guy I've ever seen, but he's also the quietest."

A sudden enormous boom of thunder stopped the conversation. The next flash of light and immediate crash took out the electricity.

"Oh, great." Angie hugged her own pillow. "Let's worry about it in the morning." She pulled up the extra blanket she'd found and curled up as small as possible.

After a few minutes, Kerry spoke quietly. "How would you guys feel about pushing the beds together?"

Angie hopped out onto the cold floor and gave her single bed a shove. It thudded against Kerry's with a satisfying *thump*. Another thump came from the other side of Kerry.

"Remember when you were a little kid and you ran and got in bed with your parents during a storm?" Kerry's voice was soft.

"No," Paula said.

But Angie remembered. She reached out her arm and took hold of Kerry's hand. Kerry squeezed. Angie was surprised at how much better she felt.

Angie had no idea what time it was when she came awake enough to hear the crying. As soon as she realized where she was and what she was hearing, she sat up and realized her hand was empty.

"Kerry?" she whispered. She felt around in the bed beside her. Kerry wasn't there. "Kerry? Paula! Kerry's gone!"

She heard Paula gasp as she shone her flashlight on Kerry's empty bed between them.

Before either could say more, Kerry came flying into the room and with a dive landed between them. "Did you hear it? I had to go to the bathroom. The sound is even louder in there."

Angie groped until she found her own light on the bedside table she'd pushed her bed away from.

"I am not moving out of this room," Kerry pulled her blanket up to cover her hunched-over body. Her back pressed against the bed and the wall. "I don't care who, what, where that sound is coming from. Don't ask me to go up there. I'm not investigating."

Angie and Paula scooted close to Kerry from

either side, bringing their own covers. "I'll agree with that," Paula whispered.

The rain had settled to a soft patter, not loud enough to keep them from hearing the sounds from the ballroom above them. After a few minutes of crying, a child's voice floated down to them. Then another voice arguing.

"I wish we could make out what they're saying," Angie said.

"I wish they'd stop. Do you realize that now we have two ghosts?" Paula said.

The three girls huddled close together, listening to what seemed like an argument. The verbal fight was followed by a long period of silence.

"Is it over?" Angie whispered.

"Maybe. I hope so." Kerry relaxed a little beside Angie.

But their ghosts weren't finished. The sound of music, hauntingly beautiful, an eerie melody, drifted into their room.

"I think I've had enough," Kerry decided. "Let's go home tomorrow, Angie, Paula. Okay by you? Let's get out of here, before we experience something worse than voices and music in the night."

"You've got my vote," Paula whispered.

"Can we give Val a ride back to Houston?"

Angie didn't want to be awakened again by the crying and whispers, but she also hated to leave Val without knowing if she'd ever see him again.

"Okay by me," Kerry agreed.

"If he wants to leave early." Paula spoke Angie's thoughts.

"I'll talk him into going." Angie slid into a lying-down position, but still close enough to know Kerry was there. Then, to her surprise, tears came to her eyes and her throat ached. Even though these were her best friends, she couldn't let them hear her crying over a guy she hardly knew.

Turning her back, she cried over the lonely ache inside her and wondered if the ghost-child in the attic cried for the same reason.

Chapter 15

Angie woke, groggy from very little sleep. The storm, which had paused in the night, seemed to have picked up intensity with the dawn. She lay in bed listening to rain pouring and the wind roaring around the old house. Their bedroom creaked and groaned as if each blast of air could sail their beds away along the beach and across the ocean. She realized she was flat on her stomach and her right hand grasped the side of the bed. She loosened her fingers, which were numb and cold.

"Angie, are you awake?" Kerry whispered.

"I've hardly slept at all." Angie sat up, pulling the covers with her, knotting them under her chin.

Kerry had circles under her eyes and her hair tumbled wildly about her frowning face. "I had the strangest dream last night. It left me feeling empty and afraid."

"What was the dream?"

"I can't remember, and that makes me feel worse than ever. I was only left with the feeling that I really want to go home today. Thank goodness we had some fun in the beginning of this trip."

"Should we try to drive in this pouring rain?" Paula had been listening to their conversation.

"We might drive out of the storm, heading north. The bad weather could be along the coast but not inland." Kerry was always optimistic.

"How long did the crying last?" Paula asked.

"I don't know. I guess I did sleep for a short time." Angie remembered thinking about the ghost-child and doing some crying herself, but she couldn't remember the sounds stopping.

"Who do you think it was?" Kerry asked. "I wish we knew something about the history of this house. Maybe someone was murdered up there in that room."

"Kerry, don't say that." Angie shivered.

"I feel the same way — wishing I knew more." Paula swung her feet onto the floor. "A part of me is frightened by those sounds, and another part wants to cry for the child we're hearing."

"I felt that last night." Angie was glad Paula felt the same empathy for their ghost. What she didn't say was that part of her own crying was for Val and the possible end of their relationship. One that had barely gotten started.

She hoped Val would leave with them. She wouldn't feel so funny asking for his phone number if he rode to Houston with them. And if they took him to his door, she'd know where he lived. She'd hinted, but he'd never volunteered what school he attended or what part of the city he was from.

Before they could get up and get dressed, the door creaked and Brandy trotted into the room. With one leap, he jumped into the center of their triple bed, licking Kerry's face and whining.

"Brandy." Kerry giggled and rubbed his ears, pulling his head down to keep from getting her face completely washed. "Did Chad send you to get us up?"

"I hope he did, since that means he's up and has the coffeepot on. Maybe the guys have breakfast ready." Angie was being awfully optimistic herself.

"Want to take bets on that? And with no electricity?" Paula stretched and yawned, and then flicked the light switch by the bedroom door. Nothing happened. "Should I get in the shower, or step out on the balcony? I'd get a better shower out there."

Wind blew the rain at a slant as it splattered against the double doors, each with eight glass panes.

"We'll all get wet if you try to open the doors." Angie felt it was the kind of day to stay in bed and read — if she were home. She dreaded packing the car. They'd be soaked for the trip home.

Brandy curled up next to Kerry, but he looked back and forth from Paula to Angie as they talked.

"I just realized that if Val goes home with us, he'll have to go down to the beach and get his camping gear," Angie said. "I hope he won't ask me to help him."

"You seemed ready to spend all your waking hours with him, Angie." Paula grinned. "Are you going to be a fair-weather friend?"

"Today, I am." No electricity all night meant no hot water. Angie decided to skip the shower and slid into her jeans and a sweatshirt.

A tap on the partly open door announced their next visitor. "You three up?" Justin asked when Paula said, "Come in."

"We're thinking about it." Paula said. "That was chicken to send Brandy to get us up, though."

"Brandy left the room on his own. He's not so paranoid now that the thunder has eased off. And he was probably looking for Chad."

"Chad's not with you?" Kerry rubbed Brandy's head again, and he gave her a worshipful look out of big, sad brown eyes.

"Maybe's he's making coffee." Paula had a one-track mind.

"*I* made coffee when I went to the kitchen just now. Thank goodness we have a gas stove. And I found an old percolator in the cupboard. Chad's not in our room, in the bathroom, or in the kitchen. I thought maybe he'd taken Brandy out, but I see now he hasn't."

"How about Val?" Angie asked, slipping on her canvas shoes.

"He's still asleep," Justin said.

"I'll bet Chad is loading the car. He tuned in to the idea that we might as well give up our beach party." Kerry slipped out of bed, gathered her clothes, and headed for the bathroom to dress. "Okay by you if we leave, Justin?"

"I can't see any reason to stay here. Unless driving in this rain seems risky. You guys get dressed. I'll see if Chad's back inside — assuming you're right and he's loading the car." Justin turned and left Paula and Angie to pack their gear.

"Let's have breakfast in town," Paula suggested. "It won't take us long to get out of here if we put our minds to it. I'm starting to feel waterlogged."

Within fifteen minutes, Angie, Paula, and Kerry had their bags zipped up and in the hall. Brandy stayed on the bed, watching them pack.

Paula laughed. "Look at Brandy. Surely you don't mind leaving, boy."

Brandy had put his long face on his front paws, and his eyes looked even sadder.

The girls were stacking their bags by the front door when Justin literally blew in. "Jeez, this wind is close to hurricane force."

"It's not hurricane season," Paula disputed.

"That doesn't mean this coast can't get a tropical storm that's almost as bad." Justin shook his jacket. He didn't have a raincoat with him. His hair was plastered — as flat as naturally curly hair can get — on his forehead and ears.

Brandy barked at him.

"Brandy didn't recognize you in your drowned state." Kerry laughed. "Did you find Chad?"

Angie felt the beginnings of anxiety attack her empty stomach. Where was Chad? Obviously Brandy didn't know either, since the dog rarely left Chad's side.

"Will you wake up Val, Justin?" Angie asked. "I'd feel funny going in his room. Maybe he knows something." Angie couldn't avoid Kerry's eyes.

"You think something has happened to Chad, Angie? You do, don't you? I hear it in your voice."

That was how well the three girls knew each other. Hiding any of their feelings was impossible.

"I didn't say that, Kerry." Angie led the way to the kitchen. "I just think it's funny that we can't find him."

Angie poured three cups of coffee. Kerry took hers in a white-knuckle grip and hunched over the counter, looking out at the rain.

Paula moved to the table to spoon sugar into her cup. She looked at Angie. All Angie could do was shrug.

Val stumbled in, looking half asleep. His blond hair was sleep-tousled. He ran his hand through it. "What's happening?" he mumbled. "Justin says you can't find Chad."

"When did you see him last?" Angie asked, handing Val a cup of coffee.

Val sipped the liquid immediately, at the risk of burning his mouth, and seemed to think over the question. "Last night. When we all went upstairs together."

"Did you go right to sleep?" Paula asked — instead of another question.

"I — I guess I did. I don't remember lying awake."

"You didn't hear the crying? The music?" Angie asked the real question.

Val shook his head as if trying to clear it as well as answering in the negative. "No, all I heard was the storm."

"I didn't hear anything either," Justin admitted.

Angie looked at Paula, then back at Justin and Val. "Have you three guys put together some elaborate scheme to scare us, Justin?"

135

Justin actually looked surprised, making his answer believable. "I'll swear we haven't, Angie. Why would we do that?"

Angie stared at him and then looked at Val again. Val stared out the window, no expression at all on his face.

"Okay, I'm going to believe you." Angie took charge of the situation, whatever it meant. "We're going to have to search the entire house for Chad. Maybe he heard the crying. Maybe he decided to investigate. I guess he could have fallen or — " Or what? She didn't know what. "Should we split up or go together?"

"Together." Kerry stood up. "I think we should stay together. Brandy," she commanded. "Chad, find Chad."

Brandy turned in a complete circle and followed as they headed for the basement. The dog sniffed every corner, every wall, every shovel and broom, the old mattress, boxes piled up. He whined a couple of times, but apparently he found no sign of Chad.

The main floor and bedrooms took less time. Angie looked at Justin, whose face was now grave and concerned. That didn't help ease her growing fear.

Justin's eyes met Angie's. "There's no place left to look except on the third floor."

"The third floor?" Val asked. "You've been up there?"

"That's right. You weren't with us." Angie remembered that Val was camping that night. "There's only one room, a ballroom, I guess you'd call it."

As they talked they headed up the narrow staircase to the servants' quarters, then to the end of the hall and the door, still open wide enough to enter.

Paula flicked the light switch, but nothing happened. "Oh, I keep forgetting the electricity is still off."

The room was dim with only rain-filtered light from the big windows. Val wandered around, staring at the decorations. "The party — "

"We think someone had a farewell party here, then left. We don't know why, but obviously they didn't even bother to take the crepe paper streamers down." Angie stood close to Val, wishing she could take his arm. The damp cold crept right through her sweatshirt and into her bones.

Brandy did a thorough study of the ballroom,

but found nothing. He finally came over and looked at Kerry as if to say, I tried. I can't find him.

Angie finally said what no one wanted to admit. "Let's face it, guys. Even Brandy knows it. Chad has disappeared into thin, salt air."

Chapter 16

Kerry started to cry. "We can't leave without Chad," she sobbed. "I won't."

"Of course we won't leave without Chad, Kerry." Angie hugged Kerry and tried to reassure her. "I'm sure there's a logical explanation for his being gone. We just have to find out what it is." Angie wasn't sure of anything.

For the first time, Angie wished the old house had a phone. Or even that Eldon Minor would come back. Leaving Kerry at the kitchen table, Angie walked into the living room and stood looking out the big windows.

The rain poured even harder, if that was possible. She couldn't see the beach, the ocean. But the torrent fell straight down. The wind had eased off.

Feeling claustrophic, she opened the big double doors that led to the porch, stepped outside. She took several deep breaths of the cool, damp air and felt slightly better. The house crouched behind her, waiting, but she had escaped, feeling she would suffocate if she didn't get some fresh air.

"I like rain, don't you?" Val said in a low voice behind her. She swung around, startled. He smiled, but not at her. He stared at the beach, as if he could see through the wet, gray screen of water pouring from an invisible sky.

"Sometimes, but right now I've had enough. This flood is more than we need. We had decided to go home today. Want to ride back to Houston with us, Val? Do you have to be back in school Monday?"

"I guess." Val leaned on the porch railing.

"You guess? Is your school that lenient?"

"I'm not very good at staying on a schedule."

Angie moved closer to Val, took his arm, and leaned against him. "Where do you think Chad could be?"

Val shook his head. "I don't know him very well."

She stared at the rain long enough to see through it, and what became barely visible was the boathouse. "We didn't look in the boathouse." She stood straight, let go of Val's arm.

"I don't know why he'd go there, but — "

"Want me to go look?" Val offered.

"I hate for you to get soaked."

"I'll dry off. No worse than swimming." Without another word, Val placed one hand on the porch railing, leaped gracefully over, and landed just past Eldon's planting of tiger lilies.

Angie followed him with her eyes for as long as she could see through the rain. He ran, hunched over, then disappeared.

Within minutes, Val walked back toward the house — alone.

"You should have heard the rain on that tin roof." Val smiled. His long hair hung in clumps. Water dripped from the ends, from his nose, his chin. Her previous fear was replaced by an overwhelming sense of love and the urge to kiss him. He looked so incredibly beautiful and pitiful.

"Oh, let me go get a towel. Stay right here." Angie ran inside and down the hall to the kitchen. She dug out her damp beach towel from her swim bag.

"Where — "

"I'll be right back." Angie didn't want to tell Kerry that Val had struck out in the last place they hadn't searched for Chad. And she didn't want to say I'm trying not to fall in love when we have more serious things to think about. How could a person swing from fear to love to guilt and back to a fuzzy warm urge to smother Val with her deep feelings?

She tossed the towel over Val's head and he rubbed his hair dry. Then he took her in his arms and kissed her long and deep. He had seen her love, responded to the emotion. Now she responded to his lips on hers, searching, asking if she really cared for him.

Then Val stepped away. "I'm sorry — I — "

She touched his lips with one finger. "Don't say that, Val. I wanted you to kiss me. I liked it."

Angie took Val's hand and led him back into the warm kitchen.

Paula had all four burners on the gas stove lit. The blue flames danced, sending a little warmth into the room. Angie filled the tea kettle with some of their bottled water and set it on the large front burner.

Kerry had her head down on her hands. Justin scribbled in his notebook. Paula studied Angie and Val. Could she see what had happened between them?

"Did you go swimming, Val?" she asked.

"We realized no one had looked in the boathouse," Angie answered. "Val went down there, it was empty."

Brandy huddled under the kitchen table, lying across Kerry's feet. He whined at them, miserable without Clad.

Angie made cups of tea for everyone. As soon as Kerry finished drinking hers, she broke the silence. "I can't sit here all day waiting. I'm going into town and get some help."

"Who? The police?" Angie asked.

"You think they'll come out here today and look around?" Justin asked. "In this storm?"

"Maybe not, but I've got to do something. Chad is missing!" Kerry stood. Brandy looked up at her and whined.

"You can't go alone. I'll go with you." Justin closed his notebook.

Paula looked at Justin, then at Angie. "I'm not sure I want to stay here alone."

"Thanks a lot," Angie said.

"Well, you know what I mean." Paula glanced at Val, then back to Angie.

Angie did understand, but as much as she liked Val, she wasn't sure she wanted to stay alone in the old house with him for several hours. He was so hard to talk to.

Brandy whined again. He'd heard the word "go," and he seemed to be torn between going with Kerry or waiting for Chad to come back and tell him what to do.

Justin made the decision. "I'll go with Kerry. You three and Brandy stay here in case Chad shows up. If we all go, he'll think we left without him."

"He knows we would never do that," Kerry said. "Brandy, stay." Kerry gave the command, and Brandy, eyes huge and sad, crawled back under the table.

The pouring rain eased off long enough for Kerry and Justin to run to the car. Angie watched them leave the house, tried to think of something to do. "Want to play a game?"

"Not really," Paula said. "Do you?"

"I guess not," Angie said. Waiting for Kerry and Justin to go to town and come back was going to be miserable. There must be something they could do besides wait.

"I wonder if the waves are too high to swim," Angie said.

"Swimming today would be dangerous." Val's voice was firm, such a change from his casual approach to life that Angie knew he was right.

Brandy began to whine at the door.

"Poor Brandy." Angie realized the dog

hadn't been out for hours. "You must be about to pop." She stood and walked with him to the front door. He wagged his tail furiously, then dashed out as Angie opened the door.

She had no sooner returned to the kitchen table when Kerry and Justin came back inside, dripping wet. Justin was deadly serious, and Kerry's face twisted into a mask of tragedy.

"What's wrong?" Paula jumped up.

"The Jeep started, then almost immediately stopped." Kerry shook her head. "I filled the car with gas in town the other day. Remember?"

"As soon as the gas in the line ran out, the engine died." Justin continued. "We checked around, but the problem was obvious. The gas tank was dry. Someone must have drained it."

"Last night?" Angie asked.

"Who knows? Sometime since we got back and found the house lit up and Eldon knocked out." Justin tore a sheet off the roll of paper towels on the counter and dried his face and hands. "I don't know why he'd do it, but Minor could have drained it himself that night he left. Remember, we didn't go out to the car with him."

While they stood looking at each other, wondering what was happening, a huge clap of thunder boomed, signaling the next wave of rain. Lightning flashed and almost immediately thunder crashed again.

"Oh, no — Brandy's outside." Angie leaped to run and let the dog back in. He'd be in a tizzy.

But Brandy wasn't cowering on the porch. Angie looked around the yard. Despite the rain pouring down again, she ran into the yard, down the dune, and onto the beach.

"Brandy!" she yelled in both directions. "Come! Brandy!" Wind tore the words from her mouth, plastered her clothes against her body. Her hair whipped around her face. She clawed it away so she could see. The surf pounded in behind her, almost roaring with huge waves breaking onto the beach.

She ran to the Jeep. Maybe Brandy had wanted out to go with Kerry and Justin. He might have slipped past them and into the car.

The Jeep crouched in the muddy drive, looking forlorn through the curtain of rain. No dog jumped and bounced, asking to get in or out of the car. Angie fell to her knees and peered under the car. Nothing.

"Brandy!" She yelled as loud as she could. "Brandy, come! Come, boy!"

No whining, no barking, no streak of red-brown fur dashed past her, heading for the house.

Angie tried to shelter her head from rain so hard it stung her face and scalp. She had no choice but to go back inside herself.

Everyone stood on the porch or just inside the door.

"Find him?" Paula asked.

"No. Brandy is gone."

Chapter 17

"Maybe he got a whiff of Chad's scent," Kerry said, with just a bit of hope in her voice. "If we find Brandy, we'll find Chad." Kerry stood up, ready to search. But she was stopped when a huge flash and crack of thunder rang out.

They all stood in the doorway of the old house for a few minutes and watched the storm increase in intensity. Then Kerry said, "Chad must be hungry, wherever he is."

Angie nearly lost her composure over Kerry's remark. Where was Chad? By now he should have returned. Angie knew that for some reason, Chad wasn't free to come back. He was either in trouble, or — or —

"I suppose we could fix some sandwiches if anyone here is hungry." Angie cut off her thoughts and headed for the kitchen.

"I feel so helpless." Kerry didn't touch the food that Angie placed in front of her. "We can't call for help. We can't go to town for help. And with it storming like this, we can't even look around outside."

No one disagreed with Kerry.

"Maybe Eldon Minor will come to see if we're all right." Paula expressed the one chance of anyone else knowing they were stranded.

Angie knew it wasn't impossible, but on the other hand, if Eldon were somehow involved in what was happening here, he might already be hiding someplace. Angie shivered.

Everyone found something to do or not to do during the afternoon. Angie was sleepy, but it looked as if they'd have to spend another night in a dark house. She didn't want to lie awake, so she kept her eyes open by playing a half-hearted game of Monopoly with Justin and Paula.

Kerry sat in the kitchen without playing the board game. She had batteries for her radio-CD player, so she kept it going, listening for weather reports or local news. All they learned was that they were witnessing one of the worst tropical storms of the spring. They didn't need a radio commentator to give them that news.

Val stood on the porch and watched the storm for the longest time. Occasionally Angie peeked out at him. How could anyone stand and stare at rain for so long? What was he thinking about?

About four o'clock, Angie made some popcorn in a skillet on the gas stove. "Val?" She stepped to the front door and called. "Want some popcorn?"

When he didn't answer, she stepped outside onto the porch and looked. Val was gone. She ran to one end and called his name, then to the other.

"Val isn't on the porch anymore," she said, returning to the warm kitchen. "Where do you think he went in this rain?"

"I'll bet he decided to look for Brandy." Justin took a fistful of popcorn and stuffed it into his mouth. "He seemed to really take a liking to the dog."

"He could have decided the rain wasn't going to let up, so he'd hike to his camp and get his gear," Paula suggested.

"He never said he'd ride back to Houston

with us, but he didn't say no, so I assumed he would," Angie said.

"Why didn't he tell us where he was going?" Kerry said.

"I don't think he's used to telling people what he's doing or where he's going." Angie knew that about Val, if little else. "Probably drives his parents crazy."

"Or they don't care," Paula said.

"How can we just sit here?" Kerry suddenly jumped to her feet and screamed.

She ran out of the room, and they heard her feet thumping the stairs.

"Poor Kerry." Paula leaned back in her chair. "I understand her being upset, but I don't know what to do."

"I guess we could be out there in the rain, searching for Chad and Brandy. It wouldn't matter how wet we got. We could have put our bathing suits on." Angie sat at the table again and watched Justin count play money. "Maybe Chad got up early this morning and went swimming by himself. Maybe he got in trouble out there and — "

"He never did that. You're the only one of us, Angie, who gets up early, and you're the only one who's gone swimming alone at the crack of dawn. Chad's a good swimmer, but he hates being alone. You know that."

Angie did know Chad's habits as well as her own, as well as Kerry's and Paula's. "And Brandy would have gone with him — not swimming, but to the beach. Instead, he came to our room."

Justin found some candles in the back of one of the kitchen drawers and lit them, setting them on the kitchen table and counter for dim but adequate lighting. He melted the bottom of a short, fat candle and fastened it in a cup for easy carrying. The electricity wasn't going to come back on.

"Did you check the breaker box, Justin?" Paula asked.

"Yes. Minor showed me where it was. That was the first thing I checked. Lightning must have taken the power out at the pole. If I lived way out here, I'd have a back-up generator for emergency electricity."

"Let's make a plan," Angie said. "Tomorrow morning, no matter what the weather, we'll hike out of here to town. Can't be much more than a few miles."

"All of us?" Paula asked. "Should we all walk out?"

"I'd feel better if we stuck together from

now on." Angie thought Val should be back by now.

"I'm going to move the mattress off my bed and sleep in your room tonight if you guys don't mind," Justin said.

The rain didn't let up. Angie, Paula, and Justin huddled together in the kitchen for as long as they could stand it. Justin didn't seem to run out of things to write in his notebook, but Paula and Angie stared at paperback novels without seeing them.

Angie's eyes kept blurring. "I'm going to try to sleep."

To Angie's surprise, she slept all night long. A dim ray of sunshine woke her, and she sat up abruptly. Kerry and Paula were still asleep, but Justin's bed was empty. He must have slipped out even earlier.

"Paula, Kerry," she said in a whisper. "The sun is shining. Get up. Let's go outside."

Angie had slept in her clothes, not knowing what might happen. She slipped her feet into her shoes and ran downstairs and quickly to the kitchen.

She ran to the front door and out onto the porch. "Justin," she called. "You outside?"

It was barely light, and the sun was just

peeking over the horizon. The sky wasn't clear, signaling the end of the rain, but at least there was a chance for a dry morning.

"Justin?" she called again.

Turning, she ran back inside, took the stairs two at a time, and dashed to the room where the boys had been sleeping. Justin hadn't moved back there during the night. The other beds were empty. Just in case, she continued down the hall to Val's room. Her last hope slid away when that room was empty, too.

Pressing her hand to her mouth, she choked back tears.

She kept her cool until she stepped into her own bedroom.

"Angie, what's wrong?" Paula could see Angie's dismay.

"Oh, Paula, Kerry." Her voice cracked. "Justin — now Justin is gone. Val, too. The three of us are here alone."

She threw herself across her bed and gave in to hysterical sobbing.

Chapter 18

"Angie, Angie, don't do that." Kerry got into the bed beside Angie and patted her on the back. "You can't go to pieces on us. You're the one who's always brave."

Paula huddled on the other side of Angie. "Kerry's right, Angie. Please stop crying. We have to decide what to do."

"Should the three of us walk to town?" Kerry wondered, trying to get Angie to sit up and talk to them.

"Justin wouldn't leave us." Paula kept talking, too. "Something terrible is happening, Angie. Someone is out there, watching us — and — and — "

Paula said the last thing that Angie wanted to hear, but Paula and Kerry talking about what to do helped her to gain control of her emotions. They couldn't sit around and wait for something to happen to all of them. And crying sure wasn't going to do any good.

Angie sniffed, wiped her nose on her sweat-shirt sleeve, and rolled over, sat up. Kerry handed her a tissue. Angie blew her nose and took several deep breaths.

"What do you two think we should do?" Angie hadn't decided on any plan, but she knew they had to take some action.

"Should we search the house again?" Paula asked.

"I'd rather look around outside, since it's stopped raining. We might — we might find everyone." Kerry had a tissue twisted into a tight spiral.

"The guys can't possibly be playing a joke on us, can they? They wouldn't do that." Paula tried to convince them all that this wasn't real.

"No, I thought that at first." Angie stood up. "But Chad's been gone too long. He wouldn't do without meals for any joke."

Kerry started to whimper, and Angie needed her to help. She pulled Kerry to her feet and shook her slightly. "Come on, let's search the beach close to here. We can even go to the marsh and look around. We'll call Brandy. Maybe he hid someplace during the storm."

"Maybe Brandy got into the boathouse. None of us has looked there," Kerry said.

"Val did, but now he's gone, too. Let's look again." Angie led the way to the falling-down shack near the beach. Weeds had grown up all around it, but Angie could see the slight pathway they'd trampled down earlier.

The door creaked as she pulled it open. She led the way inside slowly, Kerry and Paula practically glued to her back. The light was so dim that she wished she had her flashlight.

At first nothing looked out of place or different from the other time Angie had seen the interior. Then she realized the dust was off the floor in one area around the counter that was piled with tools and fishing tackle. If she had to guess, she'd say someone had been sitting there and wiggled around a lot.

"Look, here's my name!" Kerry whispered in awe. She squatted and pointed to squiggly letters formed right beside a bottom shelf that ran the length of the counter.

"Chad was here." Paula hugged Kerry.

Angie wasn't sure a celebration was in order. Why had Chad sat there long enough to draw the letters, and why hadn't he written more than Kerry's name if he was leaving them a message? Had he been interrupted? And when was this? If Chad had been here yesterday morning, Val would have found him.

A thorough search turned up no more clues, so the three girls headed back outside and down the beach.

"It's going to rain again." Paula sounded discouraged, but she was right. On the western horizon, huge gray clouds billowed up from the ocean. You could almost see the clouds sucking water from the sea, getting ready to spit it back out along the coast.

The wind picked up, whipping Angie's hair into her face. But the chill she felt growing inside wasn't from the wind or approaching storm. Evidence was building that they were dealing with a criminal or someone with a twisted mind. She was convinced that someone had tied Chad up and kept him captive in the boathouse for a short time. Where was Chad now? And, too, where was the person who had tied him?

And now Val and Justin were gone. Had someone taken each of them in turn and tied them up someplace? For what reason?

Everywhere they looked as they hurried up the beach, birds ran ahead of them, floated on the ocean, or swept across the sky. The birds were also pleased for a letup in the rain and seemed almost frantic in their search for food in the sunny morning.

Angie wished she had Justin's binoculars. To her left, toward the marsh, a number of larger birds floated and circled, their wings forming a broad V. She had seen enough pictures to think they might be vultures. She began to worry about why they were gathering together.

"I think we'd better take a look at the marsh," she said, without saying why. For a few seconds she thought of going alone, but she didn't want to separate from Paula and Kerry. She also knew she might not want to see what they'd find.

A low rumbling signaled the approaching storm. Clouds swirled and sailed like fast-moving clipper ships with billowing sails. They had less than an hour before more rain would fall.

"Are those vultures?" Paula asked as they got closer to the circling birds.

"I think so." Angie knew so. She could identify a few birds, and the ugly bald creatures with red heads and the huge wing span were on her list.

"Don't they — "

"Yes." Angie cut off what Paula might have

been about to say. She didn't want to hear it.

Before they could stop her, Kerry ran up the hill of loose sand ahead of them. She teetered on the sliding crest and stared at something on the other side. Then she screamed.

"What it is, Kerry?" Angie scrambled up the dune behind her.

"It's Brandy. Oh, no, it's Brandy . . ."

Chapter 19

Kerry turned and tumbled into Angie's and Paula's arms. Angie nodded to Paula, signaling her to hold tight to Kerry while she took a better look at Brandy. She didn't want to look at the still carcass of Chad's wonderful chocolate lab, but she did want to know what had happened to Brandy.

She knelt and placed her hand on the red-brown fur that had gotten Brandy his name. The body was cold. At first there didn't seem to be a mark on the dog until Angie reached out and lifted his head. A thin line of dark, clotted blood made a necklace across Brandy's throat.

Ghosts don't slit dogs' throats.

The thought came uninvited. Was there a connection to the crying in the attic, the so-called ghost at their house, and Brandy's death? She couldn't think of one, but certainly there must be a connection to the disappearance of Chad, Justin, and Val.

She caught her breath as another thought hit her. Were they going to find Chad and Justin and Val killed in a similar manner?

Oh, please no, no!

Flies swarmed around the dog's body as Angie stumbled to her feet and walked back to Paula and Kerry. She hoped they hadn't made the same connection.

"I can't bear to leave him there for the flies and vultures," Angie said, pulling Kerry back toward the beach.

"You want to bury him?" Paula asked.

"Yes. It won't take long. Digging in the sand will be easy. You two stay right here. I'm going to run back to the boathouse and get a shovel."

"Angie — "

"I'll be really careful. I promise I won't disappear. You know Chad would want Brandy buried." Angie took off running, leaving them with the hope that Chad was alive to care. She needed that idea firmly in her head, too. Justin and Chad and Val were all alive. They might be in some sort of trouble, but they were still alive.

Why was Brandy killed? The answer was

logical when Angie relaxed and let it come to her. The dog was trying to find Chad, and maybe he had. Then the person doing this couldn't let Brandy lead them all to Chad, or bark and call attention to where Chad was tied up.

Angie stopped outside the boathouse and listened for a few seconds. She heard no sound, so she creaked open the door and peered into the dim light. Then she crept in and grabbed the shovel she'd seen leaning against one wall.

Her back was turned to the door for only seconds, but that was enough. With a slam, the door closed behind her. She ran, tried the knob, pounded on the old wooden surface.

"Hey! Stop that! Let me out!" She screamed at whoever had been watching her, following her.

Her heart hammered against her rib cage, causing her to gasp for breath. That was the only sound inside the dim boathouse. Outside, wind picked up loose sand and peppered the sides, the tin roof.

Someone was out there. Listening. "Please," she begged. "Please open the door." She tried to keep the fear out of her voice, but she heard the waver that showed how desperate she felt. "Please," she whispered, pushing against the door again. There was no lock. Someone had to be holding it shut.

She tried to see through the weathered wood, imagine who it was out there. She tried to feel the presence, use her intuition. Nothing came to her but her own dark fear.

Kerry and Paula were going to panic when she didn't come back. Please don't come looking for me, she thought. Stay where you are.

"Who are you? Why are you doing this? Where's my brother? You know, don't you? And Chad. And Val. Where are they?" She kept her voice at conversation level. "Talk to me. Eldon? Talk to me, Eldon. You need someone to talk to? I'll listen. Why don't we talk?"

Even the wind was silent for a minute. Hesitantly, she twisted the knob and pushed. No use. She backed away, dragging her feet to make plenty of noise. Took the shovel she'd come for and held it crosswise to her body. She'd use it as a weapon if she had to.

Angie balanced the weight of the shovel in both hands, gripped it tightly, breathed deeply. She stepped forward and to one side of the doorway. "Why don't you come inside? It's going to rain. We can sit here and talk."

No answer. The wind blasted the shed, causing it to shudder. Waves rolled in, exploded on the beach, slid silently back out to gather strength again.

She counted off five minutes. Remembered what had happened when someone trapped her out on the balcony. The door hadn't even been locked when Kerry came to let her in.

Her hand trembled as she reached for the doorknob again. In an awkward move, she twisted the slick brass ball and pushed, keeping her body, her weight, the shovel poised to attack.

As if she had never been trapped inside, as if the last few minutes had occurred in her imagination, the door swung open with a screech. Curbing her need to bolt, she waited, her knuckles turning white on the handle of the shovel.

A gust jerked the door wide and slammed it against the shed wall. She stepped into the doorway. Waited. Leaping through the tall rectangle of fresh air, she dashed forward twenty feet, swung around, raised the shovel across her chest.

No one. Not even a hint that someone had been there, keeping her prisoner. Not hesitating one second longer, she took off running down the beach back to where Paula and Kerry — and Brandy — waited.

"Thank goodness you weren't gone long, Angie." Kerry stood up. "I'll help you. I have to do something."

I wasn't gone long? Only a century. Angie decided not to tell Kerry and Paula what had happened. It would only frighten them further, and right now they had another job to do.

They selected a spot for Brandy's grave, near a cluster of pink and lavender blossoms, and then took turns digging. It took maybe fifteen minutes to lift sand into a heap beside a long and fairly deep hole.

Gritting their teeth, Angie and Paula lifted the dog and walked him over to the grave. They lowered him and arranged his body to fit.

Kerry, weeping openly, placed the first shovel of sand back over him. Soon, however, she had to turn the job over to Angie. She stood on the rise surrounding the marsh, stared at the ocean, and sobbed while Paula held her.

The first drops of rain splattered on their bare arms as they headed back to the house.

Thunder growled. It was still some distance away, so a full-blown storm hadn't arrived, but it was coming fast.

Clouds churned and billowed, gray ghosts, heavy with moisture. An occasional flash of lightning sliced through the dark mass followed by a rumble that echoed around them.

Angie stared at the shed as they passed. The door hung open, the interior a black cell, a prison for the few minutes she'd been kept inside. She knew. She hadn't imagined being trapped, had she? Okay, the wind could have slammed the door, but not held it shut.

Could — could a ghost —

Of course not. She'd seen movies where a supernatural being closed doors, turned keys in locks, slammed windows, whirled through rooms knocking books and papers everywhere. But movies weren't real life.

"Angie, come on. It's going to rain," Paula called to her. Angie didn't realize she had actually stopped to stare at the shed.

"Are you all right, Angie?" Kerry asked, her voice wobbly. "Are you going to put the shovel back?"

"No, I think I'll take it to the house."

"What for?" Paula looked at Angie. When

167

their eyes met, Angie realized Paula suspected Angie of keeping something back.

Angie shrugged. "I'd feel better if I had some sort of weapon. Someone killed Brandy and — "

"Oh, Angie." Kerry started to cry. "I'm so scared."

"So am I, Kerry," Angie answered. "So am I. But I'm angry, too."

None of the three spoke until they were safe inside the kitchen, but safe from what? The rain? The storm? The ghost?

Kerry finally spoke their thoughts. "Do you think Chad and Justin and Val are still alive?"

"I can't bear to think otherwise." Paula lit the front burner of the old stove and set a tea kettle full of water to boil.

"Then where are they?" Now Kerry's voice was angry, demanding, but she insisted on asking questions that had no answers.

"I think they're here, in this house, someplace." Angie didn't know why she thought that, but that seemed the only logical idea.

They each drank a cup of tea and listened to the storm getting closer. The house creaked and groaned with each blast of wind that moaned around the front porch.

"Are we going to sit here and wait?" Paula said, finally. "I don't even know what I'm waiting for. They're not going to all three just walk in here and say, 'We're back.'"

Angie shook her head. "What do you want to do? Search the house again?" She held the shovel on her lap, balanced awkwardly. But she was reluctant to set it down, even though she was starting to feel foolish clutching it like a gun or a sword.

No one said, yes, let's go, so they sat and stared into empty cups a few minutes more.

"I'm cold. I'm going to put on more clothes." Kerry stood up. "You have to come with me. We have to all stay together."

"And we'd better get our flashlights," Paula said. "It's going to get dark early."

Those were two things they could agree on. Climbing the stairs in the dim light of late afternoon, Angie tried to think of something more they could do, some plan, any plan, rather than waiting for some crazy person to make another move.

But the move had been made while they were out. On each of their beds sat a square, cream-colored envelope, propped against their pillows.

"What's this?" Paula grabbed hers and tore it open. Angie and Kerry did the same.

"This is crazy," Paula said.

"It's — it's — "

"A party invitation." Angie stared at the colorful card inside the envelope.

Spring flowers — lilies, tulips, daffodils — bordered fancy writing that read:

CAROLINE JAMISON INVITES YOU TO HELP
CELEBRATE
HER EIGHTEENTH BIRTHDAY
PLEASE COME TO THE DANCE TO BE HELD
IN THE THIRD-FLOOR BALLROOM
OF THE JAMISON MANSION
FORMAL ATTIRE OPTIONAL
R.S.V.P.

The original date of the party invitation had been scratched out so it was impossible to read. Penciled in was a new date, March 22.

"March 22. That's today," Kerry whispered.

"Is this a joke?" Paula asked.

"How are we going to R.S.V.P. and to whom?" Kerry turned the card over and looked on the back. She didn't realize how strange her worry sounded.

"What are we going to do?" Paula looked at Kerry, then Angie.

"There's only one thing *to* do," Angie decided. "We're going to the party."

Chapter 20

As if someone were watching them, as if someone were listening, the music floated down from the third floor as soon as Angie announced that they were attending the party.

"I think someone can hear us," Paula said, glancing up.

"Or see us." Kerry bit her lip and looked at Angie for direction.

Angie shone her light on the heat register over their beds, then stepped up onto the bed, her face tilted toward the wire screen. "We're coming up there. We're coming to your party," she said in a quiet voice, trying to make the statement firm, without fear.

For about five seconds the music stopped, as if someone wanted to make sure he heard everything Angie said.

"Come, please come to my party." The

voice was high and thin, pleading, like that of a lonely child.

Then the music started again, floating down to them, a few decibels louder, the melody dreamy. Couples would want to step onto the dance floor, lean into each other, and sway gently back and forth. Guys would pull their dates as close as they dared, and the two would look into each other's eyes with love.

"Okay, let's go. That's not a ghost. There's someone up there." Angie thought she would be less scared of a person than she would a ghost, but maybe not. She didn't really want to go up to the ballroom.

Rain poured outside with the onset of the new storm — or a continuation of the last. Lightning flashed and thunder boomed, shaking the old house with each crash. The wind howled and screamed; it was especially fierce as they left the bedroom and descended the staircase toward the front door.

Despite her shaking knees, Angie led the way through the darkened house, following the darkness down the stairs, into the kitchen, and to the bottom of the stairs that led to what they had called the servants' quarters. The staircase that climbed to the third floor.

She stopped and shone her light upward.

The beam wavered, flickering from wall to wall. She needed both hands to steady the light. The staircase looked narrower than ever, more claustrophobic. The blackness stretched upward for what seemed like miles. The flashlight's soft beam did little to make Angie confident. She felt she was climbing into one of the blackest of thunder clouds.

A rumble of thunder boomed like a drumroll to announce that they were going to do something foolish.

Kerry and Paula stood so close to Angie she could hear them breathing. Paula spoke. "Are we sure we want to do this?"

"No." Angie took the first step upward. "But the guys are up there."

"How can you possibly know that?" Kerry clutched Angie's back jeans pocket.

"I just feel sure I'm right." Angie kept climbing, one step at a time, biting off one chunk of darkness, then another, and another.

"If this is a major joke, I'm going to kill all three of them." Paula tried to get angry.

"But Brandy — " Kerry's voice wavered.

The three girls moved as one clumsy being, slow to cover even a foot of space.

Finally they stood in front of the door at the end of the hall. Darkness was complete here and alive. The humid air pushed against them, while the slow, dreamy music filled their brains. Angie felt a kind of spell come over her, an idea that they were in a shared dream, or nightmare, and would float out of it if they didn't keep moving. She gripped the cold doorknob, feeling the deep ridges in the metal.

The door opened, making only a soft swishing sound, as if someone had oiled the hinges. Angie blinked her eyes, blinked again. Around the perimeter of the room, candles flickered, giving off a soft, warm glow.

She stepped inside, just barely into the room, so she could turn and dash away if she needed to escape. The room smelled damp and fishy, as if their dream continued underwater.

The faded crepe paper streamers still hung around the ceiling, but someone had added strings of seaweed as if to enhance the festive decor. Seashells lay arranged in patterns at the bottom of each candle. Most of the shells were those small angel wings or scallops, but here and there an occasional whelk, murex, or sand dollar was displayed like a special treasure. The arrangements looked like those in the collection they'd found in the boathouse. Maybe those shells had been moved.

The candlelight wasn't enough to see far into the room. Angie continued to shine her light in a circle, spotting a few chairs, and then the radio-boom box that was the source of the music. Not Kerry's; this one was smaller.

From a dreamy slow-dance number, the tune had changed to a waltz. Soft footsteps rustled and echoed across the ballroom floor as if a couple spun and slid to the rhythm.

"There, at the end of the room, looking out the window," Paula whispered, her mouth so close to Angie's ear, Angie could feel the warmth of her breath. "Someone — someone — "

Three figures sat on three straight-backed chairs, looking out at the storm, at the water sluicing the windowpanes.

Angie moved closer, Kerry and Paula right behind her. "It's — it's Justin and Chad." Angie recognized Justin's unruly dark hair and Chad's blondness.

Between the two guys — and the guys had their arms around her — sat a woman, a woman with long blonde hair.

"I'm sure!" Angie said with an explosion of the breath she'd been holding. All her fear slid away. Surprise, then relief, and then anger filled her. "You guys! I knew this was a prank, a huge practical joke. I'm going to kill both of you."

Angie led the way to the window. Kerry and Paula giggled right behind her. Paula spoke. "What a relief! I can't believe you'd go to this much trouble for a joke."

"I'm never going to forgive you, Chad Grindle," Kerry fussed. "You had us scared to pieces."

Angie never would have believed such a trick from Val, but she knew Justin and Chad had insisted that he join in their elaborate scheme to frighten the girls.

"Val — " Angie started to give him what for, but she stopped, the word stuck in her throat.

The reason Justin and Chad hadn't said anything, hadn't jumped up and yelled, "Surprise!" was that neither was conscious. Both slumped, eyes closed, leaning against — against —

The girl in the party dress between them wasn't Val in a blonde wig as Angie had thought. She wasn't even a girl — well, she had been, but — but —

Between Chad and Justin, their limp arms circling her shoulders, sat a body, her face a contorted, grinning skull.

Chapter 21

Paula screamed. Kerry, clutching Angie's arm with a death grip, started to sob softly. All Angie could do was stare at the sight before them.

Parts of the girl's body that showed out of the long dress were leathery, mummified. Arms, shriveled to nothing but bone covered by dried skin, lay folded together in her lap. Bony fingers held a bouquet of fresh flowers. Angie recognized some of the blossoms as those growing in the dunes along the beach.

Eyes stared out the window, dark hollows that saw nothing, focused only on death. Her cheeks lay sunken, collapsed in, so they had pulled the lips away from the toothy grin.

Her party dress, a mass of ruffles, was faded to old ivory, patterned with shadows of blue and pink flower blossoms.

"Those — those are my earrings." Paula pointed to a pair of pink discs hung with several pink and wine beaded chains.

"And my bracelet." Angie didn't want to touch the pink plastic ring that looked like rose quartz crystal. The circle dangled on the skeleton's bony wrist.

"Who — who — "

"Welcome to my sister's party," said a low voice behind them. "I hoped you'd come."

Angie swung around. "Val," she whispered.

He stepped up to the other side of the trio on the chairs in front of the windows. His beautiful eyes burned with a joy and excitement that frightened Angie.

Chad groaned, interrupting Angie's inspection of Val's face. She tried to find some reason for this — this surprise, if that word was adequate to describe the horror before them.

"Chad, are you all right?" Kerry knelt beside him and started rubbing the hand that was tied before him.

"This is your sister?" Angie asked. She realized she had to make Val talk to her. She couldn't imagine what he had in mind to do next, but her instinct told her he was dangerous. There were three of them against him, but he had overpowered and tied up two strong men by himself, in addition to carrying them up to this third-floor room.

Val stared at the skeleton as if she were the most beautiful girl in the world. His eyes softened, and he smiled. "She never got to have her party. Mom and Dad had it all planned. Invitations were sent out. A band hired. She was going to be eighteen. She was so excited, but she never left me out of the plans. She always thought of me, not just herself."

"She — she was beautiful," Angie managed to say.

"I would have been lucky to get one dance." Val had turned down the volume on the tape player, but music still floated softly behind them.

He stepped closer to the windows. Paula took advantage of his move to kneel in front of Justin and feel his pulse.

"He's alive, just unconscious."

Angie felt a surge of relief. Both Chad and Justin were all right, even though no help to them at the moment.

"Untie them." Angie leaned close to Paula's ear and barely breathed the orders.

Val stared at the rain pounding against the windowpanes. He seemed not to hear the crashes of thunder. Was he in the room with them or far away, far back in time?

Angie stood and the movement alerted him. He swung around. "I couldn't forget her. I wanted her to have her party. You *will* stay for her party, won't you?" His smile, the one that had sent waves of passion through Angie earlier, sent shivers of fear over her now.

"We'd love to stay, Val." Angie's mind raced. "How — how long has your sister been waiting for her party?"

"Oh, a long time. A very long time."

"Val, what happened to her? Can you tell me?" She spoke softly, as she would to a child on the verge of hysterics.

"Her death was my fault." He stared at the skeleton in the party dress again.

"How was that? How could it have been your fault?" Angie coaxed the story from him.

"I built this raft. It was a great raft." Val's voice changed, became the child's voice they had heard from the ballroom earlier in the week. *He* was their ghost, he was both of the voices they had heard. And he was the one crying. Crying for his dead sister.

As afraid as she was, Angie's heart went out to the child locked inside Val, the one now telling the story.

"Caroline was a good swimmer, even better

than I was. She loved the ocean. She lived in our sailboat. She was teaching me to sail."

"So what happened?" Angie guessed. "How did she drown?"

"I begged and begged. She was busy getting ready for her party. She didn't want to go with me. But I insisted. I told her I'd built the raft for her, for her birthday. I hadn't, of course; I'd built it for me. But I wanted her to say it was a good boat, that I'd done a good job."

"She went out on the raft with you?" Angie glanced at the progress Paula and Kerry were making with getting the guys untied. Neither Chad nor Justin was conscious, though, so they still would be no help.

"She said she'd go for an hour. Only an hour. That was plenty of time." Val's eyes were far away, in that hour with his sister on the raft in the ocean.

"A sudden squall came up. You've seen how fast storms can come up out here, haven't you?" Val looked right at Angie. She nodded and moved slightly closer to him to distract him from the guys, to keep his eyes on her.

It was hard for Angie to continue being afraid of Val, but she did know he was dangerous. This was not the same Val she had fallen in love with. This was another person, one who was certainly insane.

"The raft was strong. It should have been strong enough. But it wasn't." Val, the little boy, started to cry.

"The raft broke apart?" Before Angie could stop herself, she reached out to Val, touched his arm. He jumped back. His face contorted with anger. He placed one fist against his chin.

"I told her to hold on. I grabbed a board and held to it. It was hard to swim because the waves got so high. She said for me to keep hanging on. She'd swim to shore and get help. I begged her to stay with me, but she was gone before I could stop her. I tried to stop her."

"You tried, I know you did, Val." Angie didn't know much about psychology, but she knew what this child needed to hear. "It wasn't your fault, Val. Your sister's death wasn't your fault."

"It was, too! She never got to have her party, and it was all my fault!" A storm of rage crashed inside Val and sent him pacing across the room behind them.

Angie followed him. This was good. They were farther from the guys. Paula and Kerry could try to get them to regain consciousness.

Had Val drugged them? He might have knocked them out to begin with, but surely he'd drugged them to keep them quiet all this time.

"Val, listen to me. Your sister chose to go for help. You said she was a good swimmer. Her death was an accident."

"The raft broke apart."

"You didn't know that would happen. You hadn't built it to sail in a storm."

"She didn't want to go. She gave in finally because I begged. I begged her to go with me. And I killed her!"

If Val had collapsed in tears, Angie might have had a chance to subdue him, maybe to knock him out and tie him until they could get help.

But when his grief turned to anger, he became the adult Val again. "Your coming at the same time I came back was perfect, Angie. We both came to party. Isn't that funny?" He laughed, the laughter of madness.

Angie didn't think she could reason with this Val. She tried. "We'll be glad to help you give Caroline her party. You did a great job of decorating, Val. You even brought your seashell collection from the boathouse."

"You like it?"

"Yes, yes, I saw it when you locked me in the boathouse. You did lock me in there, didn't you? Maybe you can identify the shells for me. I don't know anything about shells — "

"I told Caroline about you," he interrupted her. "She said she'd like to meet you. She likes you already, Angie. I knew she would. You're a very likeable person."

"I'd enjoy getting to know Caroline better, Val." She kept talking, but didn't really know what to do. Val was watching her closely, and there was nothing in reach to use to defend herself if he decided to overpower her and tie her up.

The idea of being tied up beside Caroline sent shivers over Angie again. How long had Justin and Chad been with Caroline?

When did Val . . . "Where has Caroline been while she — while she was waiting for her party, Val?"

"I found her." He drifted back again, out of the room, back over the years. "My parents gave up. They thought we'd never find her. But I waited. I knew the current would take her away. They moved into town, but I came back. I kept searching."

"You found your sister's — " She didn't want to use the word *body*. Obviously Val thought . . . "You found Caroline? Did you bring her here?"

"Yes, I brought her to her party then, but no one else came. I had to leave her here." Val stared at the party decorations.

"We came up here before tonight, Val. Where was Caroline?"

"I told her she had to hide, Angie. I told her to hide in the cupboard." Val used his little-boy voice again. As if he were describing a game of hide-and-seek.

"Caroline hid in the wardrobe?" Angie shivered to think about the body being up here all along, both times they came in.

"We weren't quite ready for the party. I wanted it to be a surprise."

This party was a surprise, Val, Angie thought. It was certainly a surprise. She nearly lost her composure then, nearly started crying when she thought of Val planning and . . .

"You hid Chad, and then Justin, from us. Why did you kill Brandy?" Thinking of the dog helped Angie get angry.

"Oh, he was going to find Chad and spoil the party. I liked the dog, but you understand I wasn't ready for guests yet."

Angie stole a glance at Chad and Justin. If she could distract Val for just a few more minutes. "You locked me out on the balcony."

"I was curious. I wondered who had come to visit after so many years. I hope I didn't frighten you, Angie."

His voice was so gentle, so caring. Angie shook her head to forget the image of Val finding his sister's body, carrying her to the ballroom. Putting her in the dress she planned to wear to her dance. And this week he had picked a bouquet of flowers for her party. He had stolen the jewelry from their room and put the bracelet and earrings on her. Angie closed her eyes and took a deep breath. She wanted to cry for this beautiful guy with the guilty child locked inside him.

"I have to be sure you'll stay for the party, Angie," Val said, backing away from her. "You know that, don't you?"

"Yes, we'll stay. I promise you we'll stay."

What did he have in mind? Angie walked slowly toward Val. He moved backwards toward the door to the hall.

"You'll dance with me, won't you, Val? Chad and Justin will dance with Caroline, but I want to dance with you."

"Caroline likes you. She was so lonely. I thought about her a lot. I knew she was lonely."

"Where? Where were you when you thought about Caroline, Val? Were you here? In this house all these years?"

"I have to be sure you'll stay for the party, Angie." Val took hold of the doorknob.

Angie felt desperate. Val was going to leave. He was going to leave them up here with Caroline. For the party.

"I'm sorry I can't stay. But you will."

Before she could stop him, before she could grab for the door and keep him from closing it, Val stepped out, slammed the door. The sound of a key turning in the lock sent alarm bells clanging in Angie's head.

She rattled the knob, pounded on the door. "Val, don't do this! Come back! Don't leave us here!"

Paula was beside Angie in seconds. "He's locked us in?"

"I couldn't stop him." Angie echoed the very words Val had said to her, *I couldn't save my sister. I couldn't stop her when she tried to swim for shore.*

"What's that smell?" Kerry said, taking Angie's arm.

Angie looked down. Even in the dim candlelight, she could see the pool of liquid surging under the door toward her feet. She bent, dipped her finger into the water, brought her fingertip to her nose.

"It's gasoline." Angie gasped and stepped back.

"The Jeep. It's the gas he took out of the tank," Kerry said, moving back with Angie.

"Val," Angie yelled. "Don't do this. Please don't do this! You'll ruin the party."

Val didn't plan for them to stay only for Caroline's party. He wanted them to join Caroline for all of eternity.

The *whoosh* as flames slid under the door confirmed what Angie already knew he was planning. Val had touched a match to the gasoline. Even with the rain, the old house was tinder dry.

The ballroom would fast become a funeral pyre for all the party guests.

Chapter 22

"We have to get out of here!" Paula stated the obvious.

"How? He's locked the door." Kerry ran back across the room to Chad and Justin. Angie and Paula followed her.

"The stairs into the second-floor closet." Angie ran to the second doorway they'd uncovered. She pushed on the door. It didn't budge. "It won't move. There must be something against it on the other side." Angie shoved again, then gave up and ran back to Chad and Justin.

Chad bent double, head on his knees, groaning. Justin slumped against the back of the chair, still unconscious.

When Angie shook him, he began to slide. "Help me, Paula. We have to get Justin to wake up."

The two girls laid Justin on the floor. Then Angie slapped his face gently. "Justin, Justin, wake up. You have to wake up. We can't carry you out of here."

Finally Justin moaned, which suggested they were reaching him.

"Help me sit him up, Paula."

"What — what — " Justin mumbled.

"Justin, come on. We have a serious problem here. We need your help." Angie appealed to the big brother who was supposed to protect her. There was an irony to this situation if she had time to think about it. "You're supposed to take care of me, Justin. Remember?" She shook him again.

Angie swiveled her head. Smoke was filling the ballroom, and flames danced all around the doorway into the hall. She realized that the music was still playing, although the roar of the fire was fast drowning out the softer sound.

Kerry coughed as she helped Chad stand up and walk around in small circles. He had yet to realize that the room was on fire.

At the same time that they tried to get the guys on their feet, Angie fought to ignore the skeleton sitting with them, holding her bouquet of flowers. She felt a lot of sadness for the innocent victim of this strange dilemma.

Justin seemed to come awake all of a sudden. "Did you guys realize the room is on fire?" He spoke as if he were dreaming, as if he saw the flames, but they didn't register as any danger to him.

"Yes, Justin, we know the room is on fire. That's why you have to get up." Angie and Paula got Justin to his feet, propped him up between them, and helped him walk until his legs would support him. The searing heat and the roar of the flames continued to creep toward them.

In leaning over to get Justin up, Angie had spotted the heating register at floor level. "Here's the register above our room. The one the sound came through." She bent and examined it.

"You don't think you can get that open, do you?" Paula said. "And it's too small to crawl through."

Angie became more aware of smoke filling the room when she squatted down. The air low to the floor was cleaner. She filled her lungs. The gulp of oxygen gave her strength.

She grabbed the chair Chad had been tied in and slammed it against one of the dormer windows. The crash of breaking glass was followed by a current of damp, clean air.

"Look, there's a light down there." Paula pointed into the front yard, but rain sluiced into the room, keeping them from being able to see who was there.

"Help!" Angie called down. "Help us!"

"We're trapped up here," Paula shouted.

"That may be Val." Angie realized that if Val were down there, they were wasting their breath.

She ran to the corner of the room directly over the bedroom they'd explored that had a crawl space. Maybe . . . She tapped the floor with the broken chair leg.

She could find no opening of any kind in the floor or wall of the ballroom. Her hope had been that there might be a way to get into that closet and down to the second floor.

Another idea came to her. "The rope. How much rope is there?" She gathered the two pieces that had tied Justin and Chad and knotted them together. Both the guys leaned on the wall, coughing. They were no help at all.

"Help me," Angie said to Kerry and Paula. "We have to break out all three windows."

"Are we going out onto that tiny balcony?" Kerry asked, realizing what Angie had in mind.

"That's the only way I can think of to get

out. I don't think this rope is long enough to reach the ground, but we might be able to climb down far enough to get onto the balcony outside our bedrooms. If only the back of the house is on fire, we can go down the front stairs."

The chair Angie had thrown into the window to get fresh air had broken, as did the second chair as they broke another window.

"We need that chair." Kerry pointed to Caroline and the chair she was sitting in. She didn't want to touch the skeleton.

"She — she won't care," Angie said, taking hold of one side of Caroline's dress. A musty odor arose from the cloth.

Paula screwed up her face and helped Angie lift Caroline. Carefully they laid the body off to one side.

Angie grabbed Caroline's chair and smashed the third window. With a chair leg, she beat against the daggers of glass around the middle window frame until no shards could slash them as they crawled out.

"Get the guys," Angie ordered. "Come on, hurry. The smoke is getting thicker."

Rain beat against them, plastering clothing flat as they stepped out onto the small balcony. There wasn't room for five people all at the same time. And how were they going to get Justin and Chad down the rope? Both of them were still wobbly and disoriented.

Angie studied the new problem. At the same time, she tied the longer rope to the railing of the porch. The rope might not hold two at once, either, even if the railing did hold. If it would just stop raining, she could think better.

"Justin, is that you?" A voice from below surprised her. A spot of light danced along the broken window and the balcony.

"Mr. Minor? Eldon Minor, is that you?" Angie recognized the voice.

"What's happening?" Myra Adams called, directly below Angie now. "Is that smoke coming from the window?"

Angie was surprised Myra could see the smoke through the sheets of rain. Maybe she smelled it.

"Yes, we can't get out the door. The room is on fire."

"Wait," Eldon called. "My ladder is on the other side of the house."

Eldon was back in no time. He and Myra held the ladder steady against the house. It barely reached the third-story balcony, but holding to the rope, Angie could step over, swing down, and grab onto the top rung.

"Paula," Angie called back up. "Help Justin step over, and I'll grab him from here. He'll have to hold onto the top, though. Make sure he can do that."

Within seconds one of Justin's feet dangled in front of Angie's nose. She grabbed it and placed it solidly on the ladder. She eased down one rung, two, sliding Justin's shoe off the top rung, onto the next. Finally, with a move that took all of her strength, she had him on the ladder more or less in front of her. She could lean into him and use her entire body to keep him steady.

"Are you holding on, Justin? You have to help me."

Maybe the rain had helped him get rid of the rest of the fuzzies in his brain. With her help, he started climbing down.

"I can't step off onto the ladder, Angie," Kerry called. "It's too far."

As soon as Justin toppled off and sat, woozy, on the front steps of the old house, Angie scrambled back up the ladder.

"I'm coming. I'll help you. You have to get on the ladder so you can steady Chad. Or you come down and I'll help Chad."

That made more sense. She knew how to help him now that she'd done it for Justin.

That was what they did. Once on the ladder, Kerry swung around Angie and kept going. She didn't argue that she should be the one to help Chad.

Angie got Chad to the ground, and he fell into Kerry's arms. She and Myra helped him onto the front porch.

"Can you get on the ladder?" Angie called to Paula. "I'm coming back for you."

"I think I'm all right, but I'd feel better with you there." Paula waited until Angie could steady her feet on the top ladder rung. It was a stretch from the railing to the ladder with only the rope for balance. For once, Angie was glad to be taller than Paula or Kerry.

On the ground, she said, "Val? Where is Val? Did you see him, Mr. Minor?" Angie knew that Val, even though he'd tried to kill them, was sick. They needed to help him.

"That was who ran past us just as we got out of the truck," Myra Adams said. "He was headed for the beach. Where was he going? How did he get out?"

Angie grabbed the huge spotlight Myra held. "I don't know where he was going, but I'm going to see if I can find him."

"Angie, let him go." Paula tried to stop her. "He tried to kill us."

"I can't." Angie shrugged off Paula's hand and ran.

Did she expect Val to be sitting on the beach waiting for her? She didn't know what she expected, but she hurried through the rain to try to do something, whatever came to her once she spotted him.

Eldon Minor limped along beside her. "He's that escaped boy, you know."

"Escaped from where?" Angie stopped, swung the light up and down the pounding surf, walked farther.

"That hospital in Houston. You know, the one for crazies."

"A mental hospital?"

"Yeah, I saw it on TV. They were looking for him. They said he might come to Galveston. Val Jamison. You know he used to live here. His sister drowned out here. They moved right after that. I didn't know what happened to them. I paid the delinquent taxes to get the house." Eldon filled her in on the story while they searched the beach. "That's why I came back out here, to find him, and to see if your lights went off. They go off a lot when there's a storm."

Angie wasn't worried about the lights anymore. But she knew Eldon was right about

Val being the escaped mental patient.

"I think he's been sleeping on that mattress in the basement," Eldon went on. "I looked at it good that night — you know, before he knocked me out upstairs. It must have been him. But I didn't know about him then, or I'd have warned you."

Val had been sleeping in the house all along? He wasn't camping? No wonder she could never find his camp. And living there made it easy for him to go to the attic with Caroline. He had been the person at the window the very first night they arrived. Wondering who had come to visit Caroline. Angie tried to stop her thoughts about the past week and look for Val.

She had almost given up hope of finding him when she lifted her light and spotted something in the water.

"There, Mr. Minor." Angie pointed. "See where my light is. Put yours on that same place."

Together they had enough light to see the small boat with a single figure hunched over, rowing.

"He's a fool if he thinks he can survive in that water in a rowboat tonight."

"He probably didn't think," Angie said, to

herself as much as to Eldon. "Or maybe he did."

"I'll call the Coast Guard when we get back to town." Eldon turned to the house, the back of which was now totally in flames.

Angie was sure that was the leaky rowboat Val had taken into the foaming surf. She watched with a sick heart as he got farther and farther from shore. Then her light wouldn't reach. She lost him in the darkness of the sky and water.

A part of her hoped the Coast Guard would be able to find and rescue him. Another part hoped that Val would find the watery grave he thought he had deserved for how long — eight years? Since Caroline had died and he hadn't.

She turned and reluctantly walked back to where Kerry was filling the Jeep with a gas can from Eldon's truck.

Myra Adams put her arm around Angie and hugged her. "The girls told me what happened, Angie. Val was such a sweet boy. I can't bear to think of his finding Caroline and putting her in that attic."

"Why did the family give up finding her so easily?"

"They were distraught. They left here and moved into town right away; then they went on to Houston to try to forget. They knew Val was really upset about his sister's death, and for a couple of years they thought he was getting better. Going to be all right. Then he started acting so strange, and they had to give up on him. I heard they put him in that hospital."

"He never forgave himself," Angie said. "He blamed himself for Caroline's death."

"Funny what guilt can do to a person." Myra walked Angie to the car.

"You were wonderful, Angie," Paula said. "You got us all out of that house. Look at it burn."

Flames had devoured the back half and started on the front. In minutes the entire house would be on fire.

Kerry took Angie's arm as she stood watching. "I'm sorry about Val. Maybe the Coast Guard will be able to rescue him. If he wants to be rescued." Kerry was probably thinking the same things that ran through Angie's mind.

"Maybe," Angie whispered.

"Let's go home." Chad had recovered enough to make sense.

As had Justin. He held his head. "I'll vote for that. I've had enough of spring break and beach vacations for a long time."

"But don't deny you'll have a lot to write about." Paula helped Justin get into the backseat.

Angie took one more look before she slipped into the backseat of the car. The front balcony of the ballroom crumbled, then tumbled into the bonfire that was the Jamison house. The place would be a total loss.

But maybe the evening wouldn't. "Happy Birthday, Caroline," she whispered. "Your brother is finally coming to help you celebrate."

Point Horror

Dare you read

NIGHTMARE HALL

Where college is a
scream!

High on a hill overlooking Salem University
hidden in shadows and shrouded in mystery, sits
Nightingale Hall.

Nightmare Hall, the students call it.
Because that's where the terror began...
Don't miss these spine-tingling thrillers:

The Silent Scream
The Roommate
Deadly Attraction
The Wish
The Scream Team
Guilty
Pretty Please
The Experiment
The Nightwalker